TALES FROM THE WOODS

I.E. Walter

For Annie

Acknowledgments

Thank you to my wife Shirley and our children Stephanie, Matthew, and Eric for their continual support. Thank you, Michael Clingan, for being instrumental in bringing "Tales From The Woods" to fruition.

THE GIFT

NORA

THE GHOST IN DANNER'S LANE

WATER

MR. PHIKIT'S BRUNCH

TOM'S STORY

THE GIFT

THE GIVERS

Across the fabric of space and time they come. Like Magi, they bear their gifts openly, bestow them freely. Sometimes we know them, mostly not. We search for them but they are not to be found, their gifts left behind, enriching for a lifetime.

Look closely as the panorama of life passes by. My fervent wish is that you will truly know such a one. Then you will be as fortunate as I.

THE GIFT

It is a good half day's drive from Point Marion on the Monongahela, to the little town of Ridgeway in the North. Anthony was so anxious to get there it just seemed so much longer. A tall, lanky, curly headed boy in his late teens, he was on his first solo trip and needless to say, was more than a little apprehensive. It had taken a good deal of coaxing to get his folks to agree to let him go it alone, especially in this very unpredictable winter weather. But, in spite of it all, here he was, nearing the outer limits of the little town where Mrs. Hatcher lived.

As the boy drove thru a light, wet snow it was quiet in the car but for the drone of the engine, the hum of tires on wet pavement and rhythmic slap of the wipers. He was glad for the solitude, it gave him precious time to think. A continuous stream trailed through his mind but eventually, as expected, it all came back to Mrs. Hatcher.

Anthony hadn't seen his former teacher since he and his family moved away several years ago, but they had certainly kept in touch. He remembered fondly and well their correspondence. The letters of encouragement, as well as reprimand, they always seemed to come on so timely a basis. Mrs. Hatcher, it seemed, could anticipate life and instinctively knew what to say, when to say it and was never reluctant to do so. The mystery of it all was overwhelming but the eventual comfort it provided was priceless. The lad always thought it curious the way his mother embraced Mrs. Hatcher and her dogged, continual guidance. Perhaps mom knew a lot more about life than he gave her credit for knowing.

The young man was sure he would have no problem finding his mentor. She would be exactly where she belonged, at the little school house that she ran. You could find her there most any day even on weekends. That's where he had last seen her and that's right where he was headed.

As he drove, he glanced through the rear view mirror at the package sitting on the back seat, all neatly wrapped and ribboned. Truth be known, that package was mainly the reason the young man was a half day away from home and alone on this not-so-pretty winter day.

Wandering through his day dreams, Anthony began to fret as he wondered what their first meeting would be like. What would he say to her? What would she say to him? Would she even recognize him? Would she remember the fears, inhibitions, insecurity of his past? His underarms steadily grew moist and he fidgeted in his seat as he tried to imagine what it would be like. Thankfully, it was abruptly thrust from his mind when suddenly, he rounded a bend and there it was. Mrs. Hatcher's school came finally into view.

The light snow continued falling as Anthony pulled in front of the school house and carefully parked. Nervously he slicked back his hair and checked his appearance in the mirror. Finally satisfied it was the best he could do, he gathered the pretty present from the back seat and tentatively stepped from the car.

"Things just haven't changed much around here," he mused, when suddenly the sound of pounding from the back of the school house broke into his thoughts. Who in the world would be hammering there today, surely not Mrs. Hatcher, so he hurried up the walk and round back to see.

Quickly turning the corner, Anthony nearly ran into an elderly gentleman, clad in foul weather gear, up on a step ladder, nailing a board across a window. The man's ample white hair and beard fluffed with each and every blow of the hammer.

Anthony didn't wait for the man to pause but instead caught him in mid swing as he shouted, "Hey! What are you doing there?"

The industrious nailer quickly jerked half around and squinted down hard at Anthony, hammer poised for another strike.

"I'm nailing a board across this window sonny, what the heck does it look like anyway," he gruffly shouted back, hammer at the ready.

"But why," insisted Anthony, "Why are you boarding up the window?"

The gentleman paused and slowly climbed down to the last rung on the ladder where he could stand and still face Anthony, eye to eye.

"I'm not boarding up the window sonny, I'm simply renailing a loose board. This window, like all the windows, have been boarded up for years, ever since the school closed," he replied.

"The school closed!" At lightning speed an electric shock hit Anthony and he was dumbstruck as he shouted far too forcefully, "But, but why? This is Mrs. Hatcher's school! It can't be closed! It can't be! Where is Mrs. Hatcher? Say, I know you, aren't you Mr. Dumphrey who used to be the janitor here? Where is Mrs. Hatcher sir? I have to see her! I brought her a present! Please, Mr. Dumphrey, where is Mrs. Hatcher?"

Rightly sensing the boy was set to panic, Mr. Dumphrey's expression and demeanor softened. Still perched on the ladder, he reached out and placed his hand on Anthony's shoulder and gently squeezed.

"Say, what's your name son and how do you know Mrs. Hatcher and me anyway?" he asked.

"I, I, I used to go to school here," stammered Anthony, "Mrs. Hatcher, she helped me, she helped me a whole lot. Please, can you tell me where I can find her, my name is Anthony."

"Okay, okay Anthony, calm down, calm down, take a deep breath, suck in some fresh air and listen. Alright, that's better son. Yes, I am Mr. Dumphrey, and I prefer to be called the maintenance supervisor, if you don't mind. Now, this little school was closed when Mrs. Hatcher left some time back. The board pays me to look after it and a few others in case they are ever needed again. Students from this area are bussed to St. Marys, okay."

"Is Mrs. Hatcher over to St. Marys?" Anthony pressed urgently.

Mr. Dumphrey sensed the whirlwind of emotion and confusion rising high again, so he softened his stance even more as he replied, "No son, no, she isn't. She left here abouts several years ago and hasn't been back. But you know what, the basement door is open, why don't you just go on inside and look around and let me finish this job. And then, if you want, we can talk later, we'll have plenty of time then."

Without realizing at all what had happened, Mr. Dumphrey had gently eased Anthony along and down the steps of the basement well as he talked. When the old man abruptly turned and walked away, Anthony found himself standing in front of the door with nothing left to do but open it and walk through.

"But why?" he thought in total confusion, "Why in the world does he want me to go into the school basement? There's nothing there but dust and junk anyway."

Anthony stood at the door for an abnormal amount of time, confused, heart pounding, clutching his package tightly to his chest. When it finally sank in how utterly foolish he must look, standing at the bottom of the steps with the door only inches from his nose, he quickly glanced around as he flushed a deep red.

The handle was cold and the door stuck but with a good push it swung wide and Anthony stepped into the quiet twilight of the school house basement. He stood for a good while just inside the door to allow his eyes to adjust and decide what to do next.

Oddly enough there was a fire burning somewhere in the building so Anthony unbuttoned his jacket for it was rather warm in the basement. Before him spread a curious venue at best. The usual smells and sounds of an old, long vacant building were evident but it was the shadows and their vague movement that intrigued him most.

The lighted lantern hanging from the ceiling near the center of the room only added to the strange illusion. Directly beneath was what appeared to be a small card table. The flickering light played and danced across the surface of the table revealing a fortune in pictures, cards, letters and even a small package or two.

Dazed but intrigued, Anthony pulled up a backless stool and sat on it as he slowly shuffled through the table's contents. So long ago names, faces and scenes put his memory into overdrive. There, that old photograph, that was she, that was Mrs. Hatcher but who was the man with her? He sure as heck was no student, he looked to be her age and dressed all in army clothes. He turned the picture and read the inscription, "John and Patti, 19--," couldn't read the date.

Anthony set the photograph aside. Slowly and deliberately he touched each item on the table, examined it carefully. He strained to apply some logic to the situation, to put things in order. But what order, there was such a variety of memorabilia, what order, indeed?

The boy was in deep, trancelike, floating, distant, confused, trying to sort and match names, faces and times. Time, yeah, that was it. He knew he could put it all together, he just had to have the time. And so, he drifted, oblivious, completely unprepared for the scene and circumstance that was about to unfold.

"What d' y think?' came a sudden, shocking, whispery voice from the darkness. Soft and gentle it was but it shot through Anthony like a thunderbolt!

The boy's heart jumped and pounded fiercely in his ears, his breath stopped as he nearly fell backwards from the stool.

"Who, who is that?" he barely managed through tightly clenched teeth.

"Just me and Craig," the voice replied. "I'm Cecelia and we've been watching you ever since you pushed on the door."

As Anthony stared, gasping, open mouthed, tingling up his back, two forms emerged from the shadows into the glow of the lantern. He could make out a fairly attractive young girl holding hands with a pretty rough looking guy. His first impression was, they didn't seem to fit.

Cecelia was a petite brunette with a complexion to envy. Slender, trim, ponytail, hands of a worker, mature eyes, Anthony saw it all in an instant and it pleased him. Intuitively he knew she would be a friendly person whom he could trust.

Her partner, on the other hand, looked as rough as a blustery, stormy day. With a mop of dark, too long, curly hair framing his face, Craig had those square, angular features that spoke of raw strength and aggressiveness. The scars on his cheek bones and in his eyebrows did nothing but add to Anthony's first impression. Not big as tall goes, Craig appeared big none the less. The boy made a mental note that this guy is one to avoid when able.

"I'm Craig," the tough looking boy said holding out a tattooed hand.

Craig's soft, placid voice belied his rough as a cob outward appearance and it confused Anthony and nearly scuttled his first impression entirely.

The quaking lad unconsciously wiped his sweaty palms on his trouser leg, introduced himself and the trio cautiously shook hands all around.

There ensued then, one of those long, intolerable moments of silence when no one knew quite what to say until Craig broke into a strange, interesting grin. In playful, sing-song fashion he asked, "So Tony Boy, what brings you to the old school house basement with a pretty present under your arm? Hmmm, let me guess, bet it has something to do with Mrs. Hatcher, hey?"

Craig's whole attitude unnerved Anthony and annoyed him even more. Fact is the entire series of events since he stepped from his car unnerved him. They careened through his head like a whirlwind, he was confused and embarrassed as he groped for words.

"Mrs. Hatcher, I, I haven't seen her in a long time but she, she helped me, helped me a lot, a whole lot." Anthony stammered. "I remember how she loved the New Year and I really, really wanted to give her a New Year's present but the school's closed and she's gone and I don't know what to do!"

Once again Craig belied his coarse appearance as he gently took the boy by the shoulders and sat him back down on the stool. He and Cecelia pulled an old bench next to Anthony and the three sat facing the treasure laden table.

The trio sat quietly and mindfully sifted through the items in front of them. There was no sound but the distant, muffled pounding of Mr. Dumphrey's hammer. When even that stopped, the silence grew thick and wore on.

"Breed! That's what they used to call you, wasn't it Tony Boy?" queried Craig.

Anthony flushed at the memory, then he set his jaw, thrust his chin out and responded, "Yeah, that's right, and it used to kill me but you know, it doesn't bother me anymore. Mrs. Hatcher taught me to be proud of who I am, of my mixed blood, and I am!"

The boy's words struck a defiant tone that he quickly regretted but which Craig and Cecelia simply seemed not to notice. Cecelia's smile sent a wave of warmth through the boy and her worker's hand on his arm felt hot as she reached out to each of her companions.

"Mrs. Hatcher has done something like that for all of us then hasn't she Craig?" Cecelia responded.

Anthony unconsciously placed his hand over the spot where Cecelia's hand had been as if to hold onto the warm feeling.

"Yes, indeed CiCi. You, me, Tony Boy here and all the others who came to share the New Year with the mysterious Mrs. Hatcher," answered Craig.

"All, all the others?" queried Anthony.

There was no response. The three sat quietly facing one another for a long, edgy minute. Just when Anthony felt he could stand the tension no longer and was ready to cut and run, Craig eased back on his bench and whispered, "Tony Boy, every one of us has a story. You, me, CiCi and all the others who used to come here to celebrate the New Year with Mrs. Hatcher. Remember how she used to say, "Miracles do happen in the new year." I never really knew what she meant back then."

"Now CiCi here, she won't share her story, says it's too personal," continued Craig.

Cecelia deliberately turned her pretty head away and stared off into the dark shadows as she said, "My story is my story. All you have to know is Mrs. Hatcher saved my life." Her voice was gentle but clear and final.

"And we thank God that she did!" responded Craig emphatically as he stroked the back of Cecelia's hand.

"Now, Tony Boy, I think we already know your story," continued Craig still holding on to Cecelia's hand, "And you can tell it if you like. Just give us the short version, you know."

Anthony sucked in his stomach, pushed his chest out and mustered all his courage as he steeled himself, looked Craig even in the eye and answered, "My story is probably nothing compared to yours, Craig Boy."

Had he recklessly pushed Craig too hard? Possibly, but right now he didn't care. At this point he needed to know and Craig represented his best chance of knowing. He was tired of the riddles and frustrated by this entire day.

Anthony was ever so thankful and nervously exhaled in relief when Craig flashed that interesting, crooked grin of his, leaned forward and placed his elbows on the table. He cradled his chin in his hands and stared curiously at each of his companions.

Water was dripping somewhere in the basement and the clock-like tap, tap, tap, marked off the minutes before Craig finally broke the spell. His eyes glazed and narrowed to slits as he searched the mists for the best way to begin his story. At last, in a faraway voice he began:

"I was a real bad ass when I was a kid." Craig spat the words out like he just had to be rid of them. "I had the world by the tail and wasn't about to let go. Mrs. Hatcher, she tried and tried to talk sense to me but I knew better. I said a lotta bad, hurtin things to her. My old man, he got on me hard and ticked me off as well. So, I did what any young macho honcho would do, I ran off to the burgh, you know, to make it."

Craig's gaze dropped as he continued, "Well, it didn't take me long to make it. Before I knew what happened, I was up to my keister in swamp water. Next stop for me was Lewistown. You know Tony Boy, Lewistown, jailtown," Craig replied to Anthony's quizzical look and unspoken question.

"It was in Lewistown," Craig continued, "That I realized I wasn't so much a bad ass as just a pain in the ass."

Anthony had to lean in and strain to hear as Craig's voice dropped to a hoarse whisper, "Can't really tell you how bad it was there. You'd have to be there, to live it to understand. Didn't think I could make it, sent word to my old man, beggin for help. He sent word back, said I was no good any way, said I got myself in to Lewistown, said I could rot there for all he cared. Man, I tell you Tony Boy, I was rollin down cemetery hill and pickin up speed fast. There was no way for me short of a miracle. I felt the only thing could save me was one of them New Year Miracles Mrs. Hatcher always talked about. But I was a rotten kid and I knew I didn't deserve no miracle, besides, that only happened to prayin people."

"Well Tony Boy," Craig continued after a short, painful pause, "I was almost at the bottom of that hill when one ugly day, the kind a day when the rain don't know to freeze or not, I staggered back from work detail cold to the bone, wet and hungry and man-o-man, there it was! Couldn't believe my eyes but there it was! Lyin on my bunk, bigger' n life, was a letter! A letter, for me! I read and reread the address one word at a time, there was no mistake, it was a letter, for me! Didn't open it for days, afraid to! No one ever sent me no letter before. Couple a nights later, when all the bros were sleepin, I snuck into the crapper. There, in the glare of that one lousy overhead light bulb, I finally opened it. Was only three lines but it made me shake like I had the palsy."

Craig squeezed his eyes so tightly shut a tear escaped and gently glowed on his cheek as he recalled aloud his first reading:

Dear Craig,

These are the bad times, you are rejected and You're hurting. But remember this Craig, I have not abandoned you and I will not let you go.

Write back, please.

Your friend always,

Mrs. Patricia Hatcher

Craig's chin nearly hit his chest as his head drooped and he rubbed the backs of hands across his eyes.

Cecelia firmly took Craig's hands away from his face and placed them in her lap. She hooked her index finger under his chin and lifted his head. Freezing Craig with that beautiful, steady gaze of hers she said, "Go on Craig, finish your story, you'll feel better."

Craig turned a wistful, moist face to Anthony, cleared his throat with difficulty and continued, "Well, well, Tony Boy, I'll spare ya the long side of things and tell ya that letter was the first a many. I didn't really know how to write no letter but Mrs. Hatcher, she limped me along and our writin, it pulled me from the pit, saved my life.

Mrs. Hatcher, she worked for my early release, even found me a good startin job at the grange. First thing I did when I sprung was come back here, and I been comin back ever since."

Craig's face suddenly brightened as much as a Craig Face could as he said exuberantly, "This is where I met CiCi and some of the others. As life will have it, most of them gone their way now. Normal I guess. Me and CiCi, and now you, I suppose are the last, guess we'll go our way too."

Anthony shrugged his shoulders, palms up as if to say what, why? Still beaming, Craig cleared a space in the middle of the table. He held out his hand and Cecelia reached inside a well-worn leather purse and withdrew an envelope. She placed it in Craig's hand, flashing him that warm, half smile that so beguiled Anthony. Craig carefully placed the envelope in the center of the table. There it sat, prominently, surrounded by years of treasure.

"Remember, Tony, what Mrs. Hatcher used to say, "Miracles do happen in the new year." Well, this is my New Year and this is my miracle."

Craig leaned over and gently kissed Cecelia on the cheek, "Because, Anthony, my new, old friend, me and CiCi, we're gettin married in the spring. Ain't it wonderful!'

CLOSING

Mr. Dumphrey stood at the frosted window of his cottage located behind the school house and watched the last of Mrs. Hatcher's students leave. The young couple climbed into their old car and headed south towards DuBois. The boy who called himself Anthony headed southwest towards Brookville.

Anthony did indeed go to Brookville since he had promised his mother that he would visit the family homestead and her brother who lived there. She insisted it was to support family ties but in reality, was more intended to provide her son a respite from travel.

And so, it was five days later when Anthony finally pulled into the driveway at home in Point Marion. His mother rushed to meet him at the door with a barrage of hugs, kisses, questions and, oh, a letter. Anthony affectionately hugged mama and warmly promised he would tell all at supper and took the stairs two at a time leaving his mother standing at the foot of the stairway, smiling.

In the quiet of his room, the young traveler threw his travel bag in the corner, kicked off his shoes and flopped on the bed. He examined the envelope in his hand. There was no return address this time but he recognized the handwriting immediately. He had seen it many times before. Somehow, someway, he had known there would be a letter waiting for him and that gladdened his heart. He also knew that this letter may be the last, and that sobered him. Reverently, he opened the envelope and slowly read aloud:

Dear Anthony,

It was so nice of you to come to visit me on this most special of days. I'm so sorry that I wasn't here to greet you, it would have been wonderful to see you again.

Miracles do happen in the New Year and this year is no exception. I've heard from a little bird that you passed your exams and are on to university in the fall. I am so excited for you. Nothing in this world can stop you now.

Inhibitions, fear, prejudice, they are all behind you, Anthony, for you are destined for greatness. There is still so very much for you to do but in my hearts of hearts, I know you have arrived.

Your friend always,

Mrs. Patricia Hatcher

CONCLUSION

Mr. Dumphrey stood at the frosted window of his cottage located behind the school house and watched the last of Mrs. Hatcher's students leave. When he was sure the yard was clear he put on his mackinaw and headed for the darkened schoolhouse.

Letting himself in through the basement door, he carefully stepped around the card table and hanging lantern and headed straight for a small room at the back labeled, FIRE ROOM KEEP OUT. He unlocked the door and lit a lantern to reveal a tidy office set up within the utility room.

The gentleman stoked the fire in the big pot belly and sat at an ancient roll top desk. Grunting slightly, he reached down and pulled a box from the bottom drawer and placed it on the desk in front of him. He adjusted the light and began to rifle through the contents eventually retrieving a dog- eared sheet of paper containing a list of names and a smudgy, old looking envelope. Slowly and carefully, so as not to crack the paper, Mr. Dumphrey opened the envelope and unfolded the letter. The date and salutation on the letter were indistinct but the body was readable and he devoured the contents attentively as he had done a hundred times before:

Dec 31,----

Dear -----

Please do not be upset with me for leaving like I did. When John was officially reported missing I resolved in my heart and soul to at least try to do something as noble and meaningful as he.

And so, after a long and arduous journey I finally arrived at the mission yesterday and found the situation even worse than reported. There is so much to be done, I don't know where to begin. The building is in disrepair and the grounds in disarray. Danger lurks in every shadow but children and even adults are emerging from the country-side, eager to learn.

I'm afraid the task at hand is even greater than imagined but with the grace of God, we will persevere.

In the meanwhile, and until I return, I have a most important charge for you and beg you to accept. I'm giving you a list of certain of my former students and asking that you please, please look after them. These particular children are troubled and require very special attention.

I know this is so unfair of me but at this time, I can turn to no one else. Fully knowing first hand of your mentoring abilities, I am confident you will do even a better job than I am capable of doing. When your judgement tells you each of these special needs children is out of danger, you and I alone will know and we will celebrate mindless of the great chasm of time and distance between us.

As always, I thank you for your understanding, your love and your blessing. So, until we are together again, with love, I wish you all the very best.

Your loving daughter,

Patricia D. Hatcher

Mr. Dumphrey carefully replaced the old letter in the worn envelope and put it back in the box. He turned to the list and neatly crossed through the last three names on the page. With a trembling hand he held the paper closer to the light as he slowly read every name on the list, aloud, pronouncing carefully, pausing appropriately as each crossed that mental stage to receive his diploma. Finally satisfied, he gave a deep, shuddering sigh that seemed to go on forever. The weary gentleman placed the list in the box as he whispered, "Happy New Year Patti, Happy New Year."

From the top shelf in the roll top, Mr. Dumphrey retrieved three sheets of blank paper and placed them on the desk in front of him. He sat in deep thought for some time with only the crackle of the wood fire for company. He thought of Patti, the children who were not children any more, the mission, the time past. He thought of himself and how terribly tired he was but he knew he had one more thing to do before he could rest. With his last bit of energy, he reached for his pen and began to write:

Dear Anthony,

It was so nice of you to come to visit me on this most special of days. I'm so sorry I wasn't here to greet you----------

NORA

FOREWORD

We stand silently and patiently before the window of life, peering intently at the endless passing faces. Each with a history, a legacy worthy of reflection and recollection.

But what of those whose lives are shrouded, unknown, a mere blip in the collective memory. Do they not deserve to be heard, to be remembered?

Join me as we champion such a one who's veiled life story has been eclipsed, that is, until now. Come, let me introduce you to...

NORA

NORA

Part One

Lady of Mystery

"Nothing here," Eddie called back to his sister as he crouched on all fours in the doorway of the low attic space, "Nothing but an old shoe box clear down in the corner. Any idea what's in it?"

"None," replied Tricia, "You going to go get it?"

"Do I have to?" Eddie moaned.

"No, you don't but I can tell you one thing, either you go get it or it stays!" Tricia replied with finality.

The job of emptying their father's house was done with the exception of this one last hidden cooch and the two were about burned out on it all. Three solid days of sorting, evaluating, discarding and sneezing was about all they could handle.

Eddie moved to close the door and call it quits, but he didn't. Instead, he flicked his flashlight switch to on and took one last look, all the way to the end of the crawl space where the roof nearly meets the floor.

"Ah, what the heck," he muttered as curiosity bested and he crawled toward that box in the far corner.

Grumbling all the way, he pushed the box ahead of him and out the attic door as Tricia joined him under the lone window in the bedroom.

"Looks like a lot of old junk to me," mused Tricia, "With the emphasis on old."

"Yeah," agreed Eddie, "I'll pitch it in the dumpster."

The contents and the box were surely on their way to the landfill but as Eddie got to his feet, he jostled the container and everything in it shifted including the lid which strangely slid to one side. In an instant, he found himself staring at a picture of a very attractive young lady in fancy nineteenth century garb.

"Hey Tricia, who the heck is this!" he hollered but sis was already down the steps and gone, her job done and day complete.

Eddie couldn't take his eyes off the picture, it intrigued him so. But he was tired as well and ready to be done as he mumbled, "Oh crap, just a lot of old junk," and he put the lid back on, hustled down the steps and out the door, dropping the box in the dumpster as he hurried by.

But he didn't go far. About a mile down the road Eddie sat parked on the berm, caught up in thought. He could not push the picture of the beautiful young girl with the pleasant but riveting smile from his mind.

"She had such an enigmatic look about her," he thought, "Wonder who the devil she was, whose side of the family she was on, where did she fit in the family tree, did she even belong to us?"

One too many unanswered questions found Eddie knee deep and fishing through the dumpster in search of that troubling shoe box.

The package made it to Eddie's home that day completely intact enjoying at least, a temporary reprieve from the landfill. It made it, that is, as far as a corner in his upstairs den where most of his "collectibles" are stacked.

"You know you're a packrat," chided his wife Annie, "Just a lovable, old packrat. But seriously, you need to work on that pile. Do something with it before I have to," she warned.

"Okay, okay but look, I want you to see something," Eddie protested as he grabbed that old shoe box and shoved it into Annie's hands.

With a puzzled look, his wife took the box, plopped down in an antique rocker and stared at the container in her lap. Eventually she opened it and there was that beautiful, old, cracked and faded picture.

"Who on earth is this?" she quizzed, "Sure was a good- looking gal."

Annie turned the photo and strained to read the note written on the back, "Grand-dad's first wife."

"I never knew your grand pap was married before," she queried.

"What!" Eddie shouted, "Let me see that!"

In a minute, he had sis on the line, "Tricia, what's this about grand pa's first wife!" he bellowed into the receiver in a complete frenzy, "Got a picture of her here, right in my hand!"

A long and thoughtful pause later, Tricia quietly replied, "Yeah, you know seems like mom told me something about that years ago. She was passing down some oral history as she liked to do from time to time. Wasn't much talked about, nobody seemed to know much about her, think her name was Lenore, Nora, something sounding like that. Just about all I can tell you."

"Found her in that old shoe box didn't you?" she continued, "Huh, life in a shoe box. Bet you're sorry you crawled in there aren't you, got a mystery on your hands. Guess you're going to go through ever thing in that box, piece it all together, hey? Good luck!" And with that and not another word, she rang off.

The two sat in quiet contemplation for a long while, with not but the steady drum of rain on the roof for company. At length, Annie took that troubling shoe box, walked to the desk in front of the window and deliberately turned it upside down, emptying the contents bottom up in front of her.

"C'mon Eddie, we're not going anywhere in this weather," she suggested, "May as well start at the very beginning."

Part Two

Spring 1888

In the years before the flood, a man could make a good living working the ore roads around Johnstown. Hard, demanding, dangerous work to be sure, but rewarding as well. Play it straight, keep your head, and stay right at it, you could end up owning your own team and wagon, maybe, one day.

That was certainly in the front of young Will's mind as he deftly guided his team through the curves and switch backs on the road. It was midmorning and the young man, already on a return trip from the mine, had reached the toughest stretch of the track. The hillside went straight up on his left and straight down on his right. No room for error, no place for the faint of heart.

Will preferred the sure footed, slow plodding mules over the hard charging dray horses and that's what he was guiding today as he jumped from the box to walk out in front.

Slowly and carefully, team and drover moved the heavy wagon along the track, soft and muddy from recent rains. At length, they came free of the mountainside and merged into the relatively open, rolling country where the spring was located. A natural stop over with plenty of shade and cool water for man and beast alike.

Will blocked the wheels of his wagon securely and untraced the mules to feed, water and rest after the tough crossing.

The stress and tension relieved, the young man stretched his lanky body out in the sweet- smelling grass and was quickly fast asleep.

Ka-Whump, ka-thump, Ka-Whump, ka-thump, the odd sounds, so out of place in the quiet of the wood, crept into Will's dream-like state and ushered him rudely to consciousness.

Instantly up on one elbow the alert young man concentrated hard trying to locate the source of the faint but steady pounding. Tethering his mules to a stout oak, Will set out through the wood in the direction of the strange sounds, so intriguing they were.

"Never knew there was a farm this close to the track," The boy mused as he stood just inside the tree line and surveyed the scene.

A rambling, weathered farm house stood about a hundred paces down and away with a large, impressive barn a little further on. Next to the house a heavy clothes line had been strung tree to tree, a large parlor rug thrown over the line, ready for cleaning.

Suddenly, with a sharp, audible gasp our keen- eyed observer bolted from his reverie as a nymph-like figure nimbly ducked beneath the clothes line and popped into view! The lad's jaw dropped as he stared uncontrollably, enraptured by the sight of the striking, young girl wielding the rug beater so effectively. Dressed appropriately for the task, she was thin skirted, hair piled high, sleeves rolled up, blouse partially unbuttoned. Each swing of the rug beater caused her lithe, shapely body to twist and contort as in an exotic dance, in perfect rhythm with her swing.

Ka-Whump, ka-thump, Ka-Whump, ka-thump echoed the rug beater, dramatically in synch with the beat of young Will's heart. Beaded brow and temples burning, the lad suddenly felt alive like he had never felt alive before!

At once confused and embarrassed by his emotional reaction, Will quickly stepped backward and as the steady drum continued, he slowly receded into the shady cover of the wood.

Part Three

Livery Wisdom

"Yes, yes, yes, ya know I was raised in Pole Hollow, I know everbody out there. That place you're describin got ta be one of the Naylors. Them families been there fer years. The road up through there is named after'em ya know. Lost a ton a boys in the war, good people the Naylor's, good people," Ruben Jones rambled on as he and Will rubbed down and tended to their animals.

Older, crustier and gruffer, Will liked Ruben in spite of it all. He respected him because you always got it straight from him. Ruben was fond of saying, "Life's too precious ta waste it playin silly head games. Give it straight, git it straight, that's me motto."

"Old Sam's got some kids, don't know how many," Ruben continued as he inspected the hooves of his drays. "That girl you bin seein up there has t' be Lenora, a real looker. Troublesome though," Ruben rattled on.

Will stretched to peer over the back of his mule with a questioning look.

"Well, ya know, she's kinda sickly as a child, always smilin, never happy, headaches or somethin," Ruben continued, "Maybe better t'day, don't know."

"Now listen here Willum, you listen now, fore ya try talkin ta her you'd best talk ta Samuel. He's kinda funny that way, protective, ya know, good man," Ruben wore on, "Good man."

The two were stacking the grooming and cleaning tools when Ruben suddenly faced Will directly, stuck him in the chest with a pointed index finger, "You go talkin t'Sam now, don't ya go with horse shit on yer boots and smellin like mule sweat," he admonished. "Clean yer up best ya can. Gonna be hard fer the likes a ya t'make a good impression enyhow, heh, heh, heh, but, give it a try, hey."

Part Four

First Brush

Will stood in the run off area of the spring, well below the drinking spot, kicking and splashing water over his boots. The water felt ice cold when he doused it over his head and upper body, breaking out in chills in spite of the warm air.

Deciding it was the best he could do, he gathered the clean shirt from the storage box under the seat of the wagon. With clean boots, fresh shirt and slicked back hair, the lad checked his mules one last time and headed out through the wood in the direction of the Naylor farm.

Emerging from the wood, Will's heart skipped a beat as he spied Lenora drawing water from the well situated between him and the barn. He stood at a distance for a time struggling to put a check rein on his rising emotion and prepare himself for the task ahead. With his courage set on high, the young man left the tree line and walked directly toward Lenora, still busy at the well.

The lass spotted him the moment he stepped from the wood, but pretended not to. Continuing with her task till Will drew abreast, curiosity bested and she turned slightly in his direction.

"Afternoon mamm," Will offered when within ear shot, so as not to startle her.

Lenora gave Will an over the shoulder half smile and replied, "If you're hunting daddy, he's in the barn."

"Yes mamm," Will muttered and continued on his way, remembering Ruben's words of warning.

Lenora turned and watched Will go as he headed toward the barn.

"What am I to think about a handsome, young man who hangs about watching, and is now headed to talk to papa," she mused.

41

Lenora had indeed been aware of Will from the very first day he emerged from the forest. She knew he was there on that first day and on those that followed. Puzzled, confused and a little intrigued, Lenora smiled and bent to her task.

Will stood just outside the barn door and watched as Samuel Naylor Jr. worked at honing his cutting tools. Once a man got that large, foot powered stone moving and splashing through the cool water just right, didn't seem polite to interrupt.

At last the wheel began to slow and Will stepped inside. Samuel looked Will up and down with amusement in his eye as he thought, "All clean and spiffy here didn't come for work. What do you suppose is on his mind? Bet it sure ain't horse trading."

"Mr. Naylor," Will quickly began, nervous to a fault, "I'm William Ashcom and I've come to talk to you about your daughter. I mean, I want to talk to your daughter so that's why I'm talking to you. I mean...."

Samuel raised a hand and silenced Will, "Come, come and sit son," as he patted a bale of hay next to his bench. "So now, that's better, what did you say your name was, and you've come to talk to me about talking to my daughter?"

"Yes sir, my name is William Ashcom and I want your okay to talk to your daughter," Will responded in a more relaxed tone, "Course, I don't know if she wants to talk to me."

"Well, William that's mighty proper for a young drover who's been hanging out in the wood behind my house for days now," Samuel answered with the makings of a slight grin on his face, "I was about to come back and ask you myself."

"Good Lord!" Will exclaimed mentally, "Does everybody in the whole world know I'm smitten with this girl?"

"You have my permission William," Samuel interrupted his thoughts but hastily added, "Permission that is, to talk. If the two of you move past talking, there's some things you and I both need to discuss, but we'll let that for later," Samuel ended with a slight but friendly smile.

Buoyed by his conversation with Nora's father, the exuberant young man thanked Mr. Naylor profusely, excused himself and hurried from the barn in quick time.

Will met Lenora as she came down the path from the well laden with two heavy buckets of water. He grabbed the buckets from her hands and offered tentatively, "Your daddy says it's okay for us to talk, that is, if you want to."

Clearly taken aback Lenora stood speechless for a moment. Then, coyly smiling up at Will, she replied, "Yeah, I think I want to."

Part Five

The Beginning

The front porch of the Naylor farm house had the honor of hosting Will and Nora's first date. They enjoyed pie, coffee and one another until they were not but voices in the dark. Conversation, slow and sketchy in the beginning picked up quickly and by evening, without even trying, they knew quite a bit about each other. Discovering they were both open, honest to a fault, and searching for fulfillment proved satisfying as well. And so, the courtship of Will and Nora moved consistently and enthusiastically on.

"Mamma, mamma, what do you think of Will? Isn't he just the finest young man ever laid eyes on? He's polite, kind, hard- working, and not to mention good looking," Nora rattled on and on as she set the supper table.

"Nora, you only know him a short time now," Susannah cautioned, "But I do agree, he is much of what you just mentioned."

"Tell me dear," Susannah continued inquiringly, "How are your head aches lately? Haven't heard you complain in a while."

"That's just it mamma, that's just it, the headaches are gone, completely gone! Haven't had pain in weeks and weeks now! It's just so wonderful! Almost like a miracle," Nora blurted out as she hustled off to ring the supper bell, a task she used to dread.

Susannah remained in worried, quiet contemplation. From early childhood Doctor Ashe had cautioned she and Samuel on Nora's condition, possible causes and eventual outcomes, almost none of it good.

Is it possible at all that love can cure? That love can cure physically, set wrongs right, smooth the rough? Susannah and Samuel had covered Nora from birth with a blanket of love. Yet, the most the pain ever allowed were short, temporary reprieves and the following inevitable darkness.

But now, Nora was experiencing a uniquely different kind of love, the strong, passionate love of a man for a woman, and a woman for a man. It was compelling, new and exciting!

Susannah grasped the bottom of her apron and dabbed at the tears that glowed on her cheeks and hung in the corner of her eyes. She bowed her head and said a silent prayer for the miracle of love.

Part Six

Courtship

Summer into fall of 1888 was typical of the hill country. Cool nights, warm, dry days, beautiful color everywhere.

On his daily stop overs at the spring, Will began crossing through the wood to meet Nora. He would occasionally have a late lunch at the Naylor's. He was pretty sure Susannah and Samuel approved of him since, as yet, they hadn't shown otherwise.

At length, Will cleared a discreet pathway from the farm to the spring, one concealed and not obvious to the uninformed.

Wednesdays became special, Nora would pack a picnic basket and trek through the wood to meet Will at the spring. They named that time of the week, "Wonderful Wednesday."

Nora neither knew nor suspected that she had company on her weekly walk through the wood. Susannah and Samuel worked together diligently to ensure their little girl's safety, and they did so without her knowledge, so as not to infringe on her privacy.

One particularly beautiful, fall Wednesday, Will and Nora had spread their blanket in a high, grassy spot a little distant from the spring. The rumble and rattle of an approaching wagon intruded into their quiet time. Will recognized Ruben and his two big drays and quickly waved and called for him to join them.

Unaware of Nora's presence, Ruben climbed down from his box, set the wheels of the wagon and approached in his usual limping gait, spouting off colorfully at Will in a loud, obnoxious voice!

In a minute, Ruben stopped dead in his tracks! He raised his hand as if to say, "Wait!" He had clearly spotted Nora. Then without a word, he spun on his heel and hustled straight toward the "wash up" area of the spring. Stripping shirt and everything he could on the way, he snatched a lump of ever present soap from atop a rock out cropping, waded right in and began washing furiously!

When he finally approached the young couple, Ruben was as presentable as a hard- working man could be on a Wednesday afternoon.

"Ruben, I want you to meet Miss Lenora Naylor," Will started amicably.

"Mamm," Ruben interrupted with a wave of his hand at Will and continued in his gravelly voice, "Would that I coulda looked maybe even a little bit better fer the honor of our introducin."

Nora smiled that beguiling half smile of hers and replied, "The mark of a gentleman is not in his clothes, Mr. Ruben Jones, it is in the way he wears them."

The sun suddenly rose and beamed brightly on our Ruben as he pulled himself up straight, doffed his hat, bowed deeply at the waist saying, "Tis indeed an honor t' meet ya Miss Lenora Naylor."

"Willum! Ya coulda told me!" Ruben shouted as he wheeled about to face Will.

"Ruben, I'm sorry, I," Will stammered but Ruben shushed him again with a wave of his hand and turned his attention to Nora.

"Miss Nora, I want ya to know somethin, don't know how ya put up with this young'n," Ruben growled, nodding towards Will. "Ya must be a saint or somethin, all I can say."

"But here's the thing of it," Ruben continued, "Ya ever need enythin, an I mean enythin, ya send for ole Ruben right off."

"And furthermore," he continued, voice rising dramatically, "If this here young'n ever mistreats ya, even a little bit," as he squinted and held up a pinched fore finger and thumb, "He gits a taste o me buggy whip!" Ruben vowed as he shook his whip in Will's face.

From that eventful day forward, Ruben tried hard not to interfere with the young lovers. When the opportunity arose though, they just couldn't resist. The three delighted in one another's company.

Part Seven

Late Spring 1889

The winter of 1888-89 was harsh to the core. As spring approached there wasn't a sole in Cambria County complaining. The winter certainly had taken its toll.

With spring predictably came the thaw, the rain and the mud, a yearly occurrence in the Alleghenies. The streams were filled to overflowing, which they surely did.

The rains continued well on into May. The ground was saturated, lakes and streams swollen and cold, summer seemed forever off.

Will and Ruben stood in the doorway of the livery watching the rain. What little work they had for the day long since done.

"Ya know Willum, that big dam up theres likely gonna bust one day," Ruben droned on, nodding toward a peak in the distance.

"Ruben that dam's already gone once and nothing bad happened cept the usual streams flooding," Will reasoned.

"Yeah, yeah, but it ain't like now," Ruben protested, "It's way deeper, wider, deadlier than ever, you'll see. Well, I ain't gittin nowheres standin here jawin with you, I'm goin home."

And with that, Ruben Jones walked out the door, into the rain, and into history.

It was the afternoon of May 31, 1889. A good distance away, tucked up in the hills and towering well above, the South Fork Dam was weakening. Water had already begun trickling over the depressed center of the breast. The clogged spillway could never keep up with the constant heavy inflow, disaster was imminent.

A small stream of water over the breast of an earthen dam is a death knell, total failure minutes away.

By 3:10 that afternoon, 20 million tons of water, propelling a debris pile 70 feet high, was surging and crashing down the Little Conemaugh cut on its relentless, destructive, deadly, hour long rush to the valley below!

By night fall, over 2,000 souls would be set free from their "earthen vessels."

Part Eight

Courage Amid Calamity

The aftermath of the flood was chaotic. Help poured in by the train load from Pittsburgh and beyond. Clara Barton with her Red Cross people set up shop and did their best to alleviate the pain and agony.

The wagon master had no mine runs so he assigned several teams to the disaster area to work relief. As soon as a road was cleared sufficiently the teams were on it. Will hauled all manner of debris out of town where it was salvaged, burned or buried.

Our Will kept a cleaner wagon than most, and that gave him the distinction of transporting the toughest of cargo. There were so many unclaimed, unidentified bodies, those in charge just didn't know what to do with them. When the tragic count of the unknowns exceeded 600, a section of the cemetery was designated as their final resting place, "The Plot of the Unknowns."

Hard, discouraging, difficult work to be sure but the tough, gritty folk kept at it because, to put it in their words, "It's just gotta get done."

Jammed in his shirt pocket Will kept a list of names people had thrust upon him, knowing that he was out and about. Some he knew, most he didn't. They were not but a name and description, nearly impossible to proceed, but he tried.

Our Nora practically lived with the Relief Society at the Church of the Brethern. The gallant ladies did everything imaginable from nursing the ailing to feeding the deprived to visiting the bereaved. As it usually is, there are no words to describe their pure, selfless contribution. Only the people involved will ever know the true extent of it all and be forever grateful.

Susannah and Samuel were amazed and gratified to see the strength and resolve their little girl exhibited. She pushed on and forward in spite of the grueling hardships. Even when she pulled second shift at the hospital she remained steadfast. There seemed no end to her energy and drive.

A false sense of security? Perhaps, but for the moment her doting parents found it exciting and they accepted it gladly.

Will and Nora continued to work tirelessly for restoration. However, they eventually, sadly, stopped searching for Ruben.

"I cannot stare at one more discolored, bloated face!" Will lamented one evening between shifts.

"Nor can I William," echoed Nora, "If Ruben is here at all, he is among the 600. We must honor him, love him, but let it lie at that. He will forever live in the dearest of my memories."

The people from the hill country are compassionate but tough and realistic as well. As the weeks and months reeled by, acceptance set in and folk began to concentrate on rebuilding and the future. The dead, the missing, the unknowns would simply have to take their place when the history of Johnstown was written.

Will and Nora were no exception, their wedding date, previously set for June, was replaced by one undetermined in time. Their love was strong, they knew that strength would carry them through to a better, more fitting time.

Part Nine

Late Summer 1890

It is often said, and believed by many, that true love can conquer all. Obstacles and objections are swept away on the rising tide of love.

And so it was with Will and Nora. In late summer of 1890, Solomon Kiebler, minister of the gospel at the Church of the Brethern, was privileged to usher our two faithful lovers into the sacred state of matrimony.

A short stay at the Naylor farm later, the youngsters, seeking independence as they always do, moved into a rental in the back of the general store. It was small, cramped and noisy, and it suited them perfectly.

Will, determined to improve their situation, began searching for a better opportunity, an interesting task in the post flood era. The young man worked a variety of jobs until, in the early winter of 1892, he managed to secure a spot in one of the local mills. Working general labor for several months to establish himself, he came early and stayed late.

Industrious Nora spent her time working with the church and long hours clerking, stocking and sweeping at the general store. As spring approached, it was about this time that the two also made a monumental discovery, one of paramount importance. A discovery that would change their lives, and those close to them, forever: Nora was with child!

Nora was ecstatic; Will was happy but cautious; Samuel was worried; but Susannah was terrified!

True, Nora had enjoyed relatively good health these last few challenging years, but Susannah passionately feared the unknown. She knew first hand and full well the toll pregnancy can take on a strong, healthy body and also on one that is not.

Determined to be a positive influence for her daughter, and do nothing to disparage her dream, Susannah kept up a good, solid front in Nora's presence, but in her personal, quiet time, she regressed, and did so badly.

"And so, how is our lovely daughter my dear," Samuel asked in a pleasant tone, his back to Susannah as he washed up in the kitchen sink.

Samuel had encouraged Susannah to visit Nora and to do so regularly and often. She needed no such prodding but was thankful for his blessing, else she would have proceeded without it, such was her determination.

"Mamma, I've been through the flood and everything, I'm strong now, it's going to be alright," was Nora's mantra. "Won't it be wonderful to rear grand- children, you probably thought you would never have that opportunity," Nora went on, "I know, I know what you and daddy talk about in the late night."

"Mind, I don't blame you for feeling like you do, believe me," Nora responded to Susannah's shocked expression, "But with my new found courage and precious Will as my counsel, we are going to try, and to try hard to do things right, you'll see."

Initially, all did go well. Nora seemed strong and able, her spirits remained high. But as her term wore on, it surely began to exact its toll. All the weeks and months of constant work with the church and hospital counted as nothing it seemed, when coupled with the unrelenting demands of pregnancy.

As it will, eventually the weariness and stress began to show in spite of Nora's gallant attempt to fight them off, to stifle them.

The fateful day she finally realized that all she had been through was nothing compared to the weight of her current endeavor, was a dark day indeed. For the first time, Nora began to doubt, and thus began the inevitable downward spiral.

During her visits Susannah worked to observe Nora, carefully looking for signs of stress, while Nora did her best to conceal her worsening malady. The task, however, was becoming burdensome and obvious. The way Nora would pause while drawing water to lean on the pump handle; in mid conversation she would suddenly turn away for a time; red rimmed eyes; frequent sighs; tired expression. All the subtle signs the darkness was once again approaching.

Her husband had completed his wash up at the kitchen sink and was busily drying his hands when, after a long painful silence, Susannah tearfully responded, "Samuel, I fear for Nora!"

Susannah sat at the kitchen table, her back to Samuel, shoulders hunched, hands lying loosely in her lap, head down.

Samuel was at a loss, he had no idea how to respond. He had dreaded the coming of this terrible day that, in some unfathomable way, he knew could surely come.

There were no words to describe what he, they felt. Instead, he did the only thing he knew to do. He grabbed the back of his chair and pulled it next to Susannah's. He sat close beside her, encircled her shoulders with his arm, she placed her head on his chest, he gently caressed her face and stroked her hair.

The evening grew dusky, the light in the kitchen faded, and thus they remained.

Part Ten

The Visit

At the very front of the sanctuary in the Church of the Brethern is a private room hidden by large, sliding wooden panels. Within that innermost room is a baptismal pool and a meditation area. On that sacred day, the sliding doors are dramatically pulled aside as the minister and candidate enter through a small door at the back of the room. There, with the entire congregation in witness, the two descend together into the pool for full immersion baptism.

A quiet, holy place, indeed, where so many lives had undergone conversion and commitment. It was here, when he was able, that Solomon Kiebler loved to spend his private time. Here in silent prayer and meditation, he could purge himself of the past and steel himself for the future.

The pastoral rigors of a minister's life are many, they take their toll and Solomon was feeling them. The day was Wednesday and the week had already been long and difficult.

Solomon, secure in his privacy, was deep in meditation when the knocking at the door startled him.

"Go away, please go away," he begged mentally, "Let me have my time."

The knocking persisted, so he rose and stood by the door pleading aloud, "Please, I'm in prayer. Can it wait?"

There was no reply but shortly the intrusive knocking resumed. The minister, born to his vocation, true to his calling, cracked the door a bit prepared to ask whomever to please give him some time. Instead, he exclaimed, "Oh, it's you. Come in, quickly!"

Part Eleven

Freedom

Nora squeezed her little fists so tightly her knuckles turned white as she shouted, "I'm just a healthy, soon-to-be mother of twins!" in a loud, strong voice partly to convince herself and to stifle the freely flowing tears.

She had just returned from Doctor Ashe's dispensary where the good doctor was pretty sure he detected dual heart beats. She had also obtained another round of medication, a vain and desperate attempt to control her worsening headaches.

Although she had not told Will nor her family, that which she feared and dreaded most was lurking in her consciousness.

Before she reached the halfway point in her pregnancy, she began the daily use of headache powders. The pain had now become so intense, she was no longer able to carry on. Doctor Ashe had given her laudanum. He strongly advised her to tell her husband and family and to do so immediately!

The disconsolate young woman sat alone at a little table in their tiny apartment sipping coffee. The many years of nurturing pain had conditioned her to solitude.

Since William entered her life, however, she felt to be a new and different person, the old banished to a distant, painful memory. In the few short years of their relationship, our Nora had truly lived a lifetime.

But now, the creature of the darkness was fast approaching, just as surely as night follows day. She knew and was powerless in its presence.

Nora stretched her arms out before her, palms up, in desperate supplication. Her throbbing forehead only inches from the table as she bowed, cried and prayed, "I will not go back into the darkness! I will not drag my beloved husband and children there! I will not! God help me, I will not!"

And just as a voice that cries in the wilderness is heard, God granted her request. The pain, agony and anguish that had been her lot was, just that quickly, gone! Nora was euphoric! She never even felt the aneurysm that had plagued her from childhood suddenly rupture and gently flood her brain with relief.

As she stepped away from darkness into the light, Lenora Naylor Ashcom realized she was finally free! Truly and totally free!

Part Twelve

Afterglow

It was now a full month since Nora's passing. A month of reflection, prayer and tears.

Susannah, Samuel and William sat stoically in the Naylor's dimly lit parlor. The tears were dried, all that remained were the red rimmed eyes and drawn faces. The low, slow ticking of the mantle clock the only sound as the three waited patiently, resignedly.

Opposite them, Solomon Kiebler reclined in a large wingback chair that threatened to swallow him up. Eyes lightly closed, brow furrowed in concentration, lips parted slightly as if prepared to speak.

Solomon had waited what he considered a reasonable amount of time before arranging the meeting. Above all, he needed clear, uncluttered minds to receive what had been prepared for them.

Time wore on as the good man worked and struggled mentally, in an effort to frame the missive properly, to get it right and true.

"Hello my dearest mother and father," Solomon's words shattered the stillness in the quiet room and sent chills through the recipients.

"There is nothing more you can do for me that you haven't already done," he continued. "The precious blanket of love you so wrapped around and cuddled me in, is that which sustained me these many difficult years. I am, and always will be grateful. Please rest comfortably and assured that every ounce of love you bestowed on me, I return to you as well. Please, let the memory of me be a happy one."

"Hello to you my dearest husband William," Solomon continued, still slumping in the big wingback, eyes not but slits, arms lying loosely at his sides. "You must know, my dearest, that you made my life complete, since I've told you often enough. The poet says it is not how long you live, but how well. We certainly proved that, didn't we?"

"We were a flame that burned brightly, for but a time. It will forever burn in my memory, may it be for you as well," Solomon trailed off.

"And now my dearest family," the messenger continued, "You may hold me, you may grieve for me, but only for a little. No markers cast in bronze or chiseled stone do I desire. Think of me fondly, I will know, and that will be enough. Promise that you will let me go, that I may be on my way. Wish me well on my journey. Through the boundless, infinite love that God has bestowed upon me, I wish you happiness, and all the very best life has to offer, Nora."

There was nothing left to say. Solomon had delivered the messages just as he had avowed. Totally exhausted from the effort, the good man struggled to his feet. He had one last thing to do to complete his promised task.

On wobbly legs he went from window to window raising blinds and opening curtains till the entire house was flooded with light.

With that, and one significant backward glance and nod, he was gone.

Afterword

"Wait a minute, wait a minute," Tricia protested, "You got all that from out of that little shoe box?

She had just finished reading Eddie's touching rendition of "Nora" and was experiencing doubt, "Where did you get all that detail?"

"Well," Eddie acknowledged, "I did some research but, true to her nature, Nora left little behind when she embarked on her journey."

"So," Tricia fussed, "Where did you get it then?"

"She helped me," Eddie replied quietly, "I asked, and she responded. Annie said Nora finally wanted her story told. I believed her."

Eddie picked up Nora's picture, that which had launched his quest. He stared at the beautiful image, creased, faded, full of history and intrigue.

"She wanted her story told," he mused, "And so, we have."

THE GHOST IN DANNER'S LANE

FOREWORD

What shall we say about the ghostly apparitions and frightening sounds which creep from the netherworld to stalk the dark of night? Do they lie only in the fertile fields of the mind, or rather, is it possible that one's perception truly becomes his reality?

Come, let us seek it out as we follow our intrepid, young heroines as they pursue and are pursued by:

THE GHOST IN DANNER'S LANE.

THE GHOST IN DANNER'S LANE

Part One

"Is not!" shouted Emma on the top of her lungs.

"Is to!" replied Billy smugly.

"Ees not!" insisted Esmeralda in her best accented English.

"Is to," replied Billy with a grin he simply could not hide.

"No, no, no!" the girls wailed in unison as they clamped hands over ears and stomped their feet, "There are no such things as ghosts!"

Billy Seger gave Esmeralda Longtimer and Emma Newly a sly, side long glance as he chuckled and said, "Look girls, your folks have told you there are no ghosts cause they just don't want you to be scared. That's okay, you know, but I'm telling you two, right here and now, there is a ghost in Danner's Lane!"

The three were standing at the head of Danner's lane looking down the whole, long way of the single track, grassy road. The unkempt bushes encroached either side and the over grown trees gave a shaded, tunnel like look to the scene. It was a good fifty paces to the end and there staring back at them was an old, ramshackle, abandoned farm house, silent, ancient and eerie looking.

It was said that the Danner's once lived there. There were all manner of rumors about the Danners but nobody really knew very much about them. Where had they come from, what were they like, whom were their friends, why or when did they leave? They seemed a somewhat secretive clan, indeed. All anyone knew for sure was that one day they were here and then, they were gone. The decaying house and overgrown gardens had been deserted now for a long, long time.

The mystery of it all made it ripe for all sorts of wild and strange stories that persisted.

Billy cunningly smiled at Emma and Esmeralda, this is just what he had hoped for. He rightly guessed that the girls were a little bit afraid by now, and leaning his way, so he jumped at the chance, popped himself in the chest with his thumb and said, "Now, you two don't have a thing to worry about you know, cause I'm here, I'll protect you!"

"We don't need no protection thank you, we can take care of ourselves!" they shouted, with a shake of their pretty heads. "Besides, supposing, just supposing now there was a ghost there, what the heck would you do anyway? You're just a kid, a kid like us. Imagine now there is a ghost there, even though we all know there is no such thing, never has been, never will be, what would you do if there was?"

Billy grinned, "Well, I may be just a kid but I'm certainly not like you two. First of all, I'm not scared of no ghost like you are and second I know how to handle one."

"Aww you're crazy," the girls laughed with a wave of the hand, "You don't know any more than we do and that's for sure!"

"Well, you can think that if you want, no skin off my nose. But last summer I walked all the way over to Hogback Mountain to see an old hermit man who lives there."

"What ever for," asked tiny Esmeralda, "Why you go there?"

Billy smiled that clever smile of his and replied, "That old man has secrets, lots and lots of secrets."

"So what," the girls responded, "what's that got to do with anything any- way?"

"Well girls," said Billy still smiling, "I made him tell em to me, all of em."

"Aww, you're full of it," blurted Emma, "What secrets anyway?"

Billy had that smug, cool look on his face again as he said, "You'll see girls, you'll see on Halloween, when the ghosts come out! They'll come out FOR YOU AND YOU, HA, HA, HA! Oh look, here comes the school bus."

Part Two

On Sunday of that very same week, the Longtimers, along with their beautiful, adopted daughter diminutive, dark eyed Esmeralda, met the Newlys and their vivacious, blond haired Emma. The lot of them spent the morning together at the little country chapel down by the creek. Refreshed and rejuvenated, they hurried home to change into relaxing clothes and pack a delicious picnic basket.

Situated just where the Longtimer's sprawling farm touches the Newly's moderate country estate is an Eden-like spot indeed, complete with a stream and stone fireplace. Everyone and everything loaded into Mr. Longtimer's stake body truck and bumped and rattled out across the pasture. There they all went to roast some fresh corn, picnic together and just enjoy one another's company.

The fall air was very crisp and it felt so good to stand up close to the fire where all the cooking was going on and enjoy the good smells that were wafting about.

The conversation was moving smoothly and easily from person to person, with subjects ranging from farming to banking to school work to cooking, all in a genial manner. Until, that is, inquisitive Emma, with Esmeralda's prodding, brought up the question of Danner's Lane. Then, it got very quiet, and for a long while, with nothing but the ripple of the brook and rattle of dry leaves in the air to break the stillness.

Nobody knew quite how to respond or what's best to say until Mrs. Newly finally spoke up, "Why ask about that old place," she asked in her calm and quiet way.

And so, the girls, in a torrent, blurted out all that Billy Seger had told them of the Danners and the old house sitting at the end of the eerie, mysterious lane.

There followed a long, uncomfortable silence as the group glanced from one to another wondering who would take up the thread. Finally, Mr. Longtimer shifted his gaze out across the field and with a far-away look in his eye spoke up, "Granted folks, some strange things have been said about Danner's Lane ever since I can remember, even as a boy. Believe me though there are no ghosts there."

"No, no," said Mr. Newly, "We haven't been here that long but even I know there are no ghosts, not there nor anywhere. Billy is a decent kid, he is only trying to spook you two and it's just for fun, that's all, Halloween is coming."

"I no like hes idée of fun," replied Esmeralda, dark eyes drawn to a squint.

"Me neither," echoed a rosy cheeked Emma.

Mrs. Longtimer had said little up to this point but now she felt it was her time. She took each of the girl's hands in hers and pulled them close as she said, "All three of you walk by that old place every single day to and from the school bus stop don't you?"

With curls a wagging the girls nodded enthusiastically.

"Now, we know, we all know, there is no such thing as a ghost," Mrs. Longtimer continued, "But just supposing now, just supposing a big ugly ghost did emerge from Danner's Lane and Billy Seger stepped up and flat chased it away, what would you think?"

The girls shrugged their shoulders and stared wide eyed at one another for a full minute. Finally, Esmeralda, head tipped to the side in concentration, spoke up, "I would thenk Billy ees very brave boy."

"Yeah, yeah me too," chimed in an eager Emma.

Mrs. Longtimer smiled and replied, "You know what? Me too, and that's exactly what clever Billy wants us to think. Now remember ladies, there are no ghosts anyway. This is Billy's little ruse. He wants to stand tall in your eyes. Just a harmless, little ruse, that's all."

Part Three

The always beautiful fall days passed too quickly by and before you could say, "October gone," it was Halloween eve. Twilight was slowly approaching when the old school bus ground to a halt and Emma, Billy and Esmeralda all got off and began walking toward home. The air was virtually electric because it was Halloween and everyone knew exciting, thrilling things happened on Halloween.

When they reached the head of Danner's Lane, the girls made to move quickly by. But Billy, who was walking slightly ahead stopped, so even though they didn't want to, they did as well. Billy stood stone still and stared, then he positively glared down the darkly shaded lane at that old mysterious farm house. Suddenly, he dropped his school bag plop on the ground, carefully reached behind a large red-tip bush and pulled out a long, slender, curious looking stick.

"What ees that," asked Esmeralda, her pretty face scrunched in query.

"Yeah," echoed Emma, throwing her hands in the air, "What the heck's the stick for?"

Billy, conscious now of his audience, twirled the stick in his hand a few times for effect, letting curiosity build. Suddenly he swung the stick in a circular motion around and around his head. Ssswissshhh-hummmm, Ssswissshhh-hummmm, the exotic stick sung beautifully in Billy's hand.

He stopped and held the mysterious wand admiringly out in front of him as he said, "This, girls, may look like it, but it sure as heck ain't no way an ordinary stick. You remember the old hermit man on Hogback Mountain. Well, like I told ya before, he knows secrets, lots and lots of secrets. One day last summer, me and him, we sat around a fire at the mouth of his cave, we sat and talked all night and he told em to me. You're looking at one of em right now. This here girls, is none other than a real, honest-to-goodness, boney fide, tried and proven ghost chaser!" Billy said it proudly as he lovingly held the magic stick out in front of him and tipped his tousled head in deference.

Now, this ghost chaser was very impressive and authentic looking, indeed. A crowd poser under any circumstances. The clever boy had searched out along the creek bank till he found a very long, lithe willow branch. Carefully skinning off all of the bark with his pocket knife, and not cutting too deeply, he rubbed the stick with sand and water from the creek bed till it shined a dazzling white. Then, so as not to get stuck, he very carefully drilled a hole in large, spiny sweet gum burr and fastened it to the slender, narrow tip. Lastly, he wrapped heavy twine around and around the thick end with a hanging wrist loop to prevent slippage, forming a good grip handle.

Then, and only then, Billy closed his eyes and reverently chanted the hermit's secret magical verse:

SECRETS OLD

SECRETS NEW

COME ALIVE

I WILL YOU.

YOUR POWER TO CHALLENGE

GOBLIN AND GHOST

I WILL COMMAND

AS HOST OF THE MOST.

All in all, folks, if you believed in ghosts, goblins and ghost chasers, you would most certainly believe in Billy's magic stick, it was that down- right impressive. And when he slashed the air above his head and it eerily sang: Ssswissshhh-hummmm, Ssswissshhh-hummmm, man oh man, it was really something!

"Stand back girls! Don't go any further down this most dangerous lane! You all leave this to me, I'll handle it! I don't want anyone gettin hurt cept the miserable ghost down there!" warned Billy as he pointed his mace towards the dilapidated house at the end of the road.

And with that, he pooched out his chest, his eyes narrowed to angry slits, his lips got tight in a challenging frown and he began to move slowly and carefully, step, by step, by cautious step, down that spooky old road.

Glancing furtively from side to side with each and every move, the brave boy continued his steady approach towards that hideous, old house. It was so deadly quiet it made your ears ring. There was not a single sound except a loose shutter tapping gently in the evening breeze. It seemed to be saying: It's Halloween, something eerie, spinetingling and dreadful is about to happen, and happen soon!

And happen it did! The stalwart lad was near the end of the road and directly in front of that old haunted house when it did happen. To the left side of the lane and from behind an ancient, gnarled oak tree appeared, a ghost! For real! It emerged silently and seemingly out of nowhere! The creature was covered in white from head to toe with nothing but eye holes glowing! It kind of floated right out in front of Billy, slowly and menacingly raised its arms and wailed, BOOOOOOOO!

Billy, most assuredly, should have been petrified with fear. Instead, he took one step backward and glanced over his shoulder to make sure the girls were avidly watching. Then, knowing that this was his moment, his moment in the sun, he raised that glorious magic scepter in the air and swung it around and around his head. Ssswissshhh-hummmm, Ssswissshhh-hummmm, the magic stick sang eerily in the cool twilight.

Now, although he certainly should have been, Billy was not the least bit afraid of that scary ghost. It wasn't because he was brave and it wasn't because he had his ghost chaser securely in his hand. No, no, the boy wasn't afraid because he and he alone knew that the threatening creature was not really a ghost at all! It was none other than a boy to whom he had given a quarter, to dress up and pretend to be a ghost, all to support his little ruse.

But now and for all time, there he stood, firm, heroic and tall, ghost chaser whirling about his head, swishing and humming as he chanted:

BATS'N RATS'N MOUSE

74

FILET,

WILL GET YOU TOO IF YOU SHOULD

STAY.

BEST BE GONE FROM HERE

TODAY!

Suddenly, the now panicky ghost screamed, "BOOOOOOOO!" and abruptly turned and ran to the back of the house, sprinted across a field, jumped clean over a broke- down fence, slogged and splashed through a little creek and charged into the woods wailing, "BOOOOOOOO," all the while.

Billy huffed and puffed himself up bigger than life as he shouted at the fleeing ghost, "AND DON'T YOU EVER COME BACK TO BOTHER MY FRIENDS OR YOU'LL HAVE TO DEAL WITH ME!"

When the echo of the last booooo had died away and the evening was still and calm, our brave young Billy proudly turned to his captive audience, still standing at the head of Danner's Lane. For their benefit, he struck a triumphant pose, feet spread at shoulder width, arms high overhead, ghost chaser in hand, an ear to ear monkey grin on his face and exclaimed, "TADAAAAA!"

Curiously, the girls didn't move. They didn't rush down the lane, as expected and give him a big, warm, congratulatory hug and tell him how wonderfully brave he was. In fact, they didn't say anything, nothing at all, at least not to him. Instead they were talking among themselves and pointing his way.

"TADAAAAA!" Billy tried a second time, still grinning, still holding his best triumphant pose.

This time the girls did say something but certainly not what Billy wanted or expected to hear. The two were jumping up and down now, shouting and gesturing wildly toward the old house! Deflated and thoroughly confused the lad slowly turned to face the house, the grin fading from his face.

It was then that he saw what the girls had seen. Something moved! Something inside the house moved! It glided right across the open window! Wait, see, there it was again! And was that just wind through the trees and eaves, or did he actually hear: Billyyy Seeegerr, Billyyy Seeegerr.

The poor befuddled lad stood where he was and stared, more perplexed than fearful. When fear did come, it didn't come slowly, it literally jumped all over Billy! With the loud click of the door latch and the moan of the ancient, rusty hinges, the hair on his head stood straight up if you can imagine such a thing, chills ran up and down his spine, his legs trembled and he felt like skedaddling, but he didn't.

"Gotta be brave, gotta be strong," he muttered rapidly over and over under his breath. The encouraging thoughts were good, and the words bolstered his stance but they all went up in a whiff and puff, gone in a split second when, with a long ugly screech, the door swung wide, the knob banged against the wall and, man oh man, there it was! Holy Shamolies, there it was! There, framed in the doorway hovered the biggest, ugliest, scariest sight young Billy Seger had ever laid eyes on!

The thing was huge, it filled the entire web clogged opening, top to bottom, side to side! The monster was completely covered in a dirty, patchy white except for the head and hands. The hands were weird, bony looking appendages hanging loosely at its sides, the fingers stretched out menacingly. Those hands now slowly came up, dragging the spiders, webs and cobs along with them and grasped each side of the large, grossly misshapen head. With a quick twist, the thing jerked off its own head and held it out in front, turning it slowly from side to side as though it was searching. There was a crooked, wicked grin on its face and fire danced from its eyes and spit from its mouth! The head stopped moving now and was staring directly at the petrified lad as it moaned, "Billyy Seeegerrr, Billyy Seeegerrr!"

Poor Billy stood transfixed. You couldn't have moved him with a stick of dynamite. His mouth dropped open, jaw nearly hitting his chest, eyes bugged out and welled up in tears and snot flew from his nose!

But the worst was to come when the thing shuffled across the porch, and stumbled down the steps, heading straight for him, holding its head in its hands and wailing, "Billyy Seeegerrr, Billyy Seeegerrr." And with that, right then and there, Billy wet his pants, spun on his heels and tore out the lane shouting, "Aieeeeee, mamaaaa!"

"Billy, Billy, use your ghost chaser, use your ghost chaser!" the girls shouted on the top of their lungs. But it was to no avail as a wild-eyed Billy, head tipped back, knees and elbows pumping high and furiously, approached the girls on a dead run!

When he reached the head of the lane the poor boy never slowed but ran smack between the girls, sending them reeling and knocking them flat! He threw his magic stick at their feet and headed down the road toward home screaming, "Aieeeeee, mamaaaa!" all the way down and out of sight.

Billy Seger, their would-be protector, was long gone now but the monster certainly was not! Steadily but surely, it was still coming, step by step by frightening step, getting closer and closer to our heroines. Emma and Esmeralda gaped at one another, fear and confusion shining in their eyes. Then, as though driven by the same thought, together they reached down and snatched up that glorious magic stick, the ghost chaser. With both clinging tightly to the handle, they slashed the air above their heads, Ssswissshhh-hummmm, Sswisshhh-hummmm, as they frantically shouted all they could remember of Billy's chant, "BATS N RATS N CATS N HATS, GHOST BE GONE, GHOST BE SCAT!"

Suddenly, something odd happened. Without warning, the huge, ugly, threatening monster faltered and then stopped, right there in the grassy middle of Danner's Lane! Teetering for a moment, it dropped its ghastly head to the ground! The abominable thing rolled and rolled over and over till it bumped to a stop at the girl's feet, grinning and staring up at them! Another moment of uncertainty and with a terrible gurgle and cry the giant beast collapsed in a heap directly in front of Emma and Esmeralda who were still jumping up and down, to and fro, whirling the magic stick and chanting!

The thing lay quiet and still for a long minute then began to thrash violently about. Look, look, there's a leg and another, wait there's three, no four! Four legs! Now arms began to appear, one, three and four! And what's more heads, two of them! Two heads!

The intense scene continued wildly! And when the flailing, writhing, shouting and commotion was over, there amid a pile of rumpled canvas, sticks and pumpkin sat Mr. Longtimer and Mr.

Newly, grinning like foxes in the hen house! "Boooo, boooo," the two whispered gently.

And with that, like popping a pin a balloon, the tension vanished and Esmeralda jumped in Mr. Longtimer's lap and Emma grabbed Mr. Newly by the neck and they all rolled in the grass and laughed and laughed and laughed!

The four hugged and frolicked for what seemed like forever and it was nearly dark when they finally gathered the canvas, the book bags and the ghost chaser and headed out the lane, and down the dusty road to home.

"What should we do with the magic stick and Billy's books?" the girls asked.

"I'll keep the ghost chaser in the barn," Mr. Longtimer replied, "I've kinda taken a liking to it."

"Oh, and I'll see that Billy's book bag gets home, we'll say he just forgot it somewhere," offered Mr. Newly.

"And by the way girls, let's just keep this little episode to ourselves," the men suggested. "Billy doesn't need any more embarrassment. Wouldn't serve any purpose and besides, he is going to look up to you as two brave young ladies, best to just let it lie."

AFTERWORD

And so, now you know the story of the ghost in Danner's Lane. Fear not, we have put this tale to a definite and final rest.

Or have we? As our valiant young heroines walk away in the early moon light, holding tightly their father's hands, talking and laughing as they go, they cast not a single backward glance. But if they had chanced one last look down the darkened road and the old house gleaming in the night light at the end, they might have seen something move. If they looked closely, they might see something move silently, furtively, right past the open window. See, there it is again........

WATER

FOREWORD

This is the story of a crusade. A real-life drama of a family's struggle for one of life's most precious commodities and the radical steps they took in their pursuit.

If you are at all familiar with the hill country of the Alleghenies you will understand the nature of the problems they faced. You will also know the determined temperament of the people involved.

Come, join me in the telling, and the countryside will once again become vibrant and the people alive as we follow them in their dogged quest for:

WATER.

WATER

Part One

The Quest

"DIGGGGGG HEREEEEEE!" bellowed Grandpa as he feverishly pointed a jittery, agitated index finger to the ground at his feet. These were the first words spoken in over an hour and they caused electric tinglings straight up my back right to the nape of my neck!

We had been at it since daybreak, following Grandpa in a wild chase all over the hillside, just waiting and waiting for him to tell his secret!

The morning was just coming on when the whole gang of us gathered in front of Grandpa's rambling, unpainted farm house set deep in the cove. This far up the mountain mornings are cool and we shivered a little waiting for him to appear. The tantalizing smell of bacon and coffee was in the air, guess that was the reason Pap wouldn't let us near the house. So, we shuffled our feet, beat our arms and played grab-at to keep warm while Pap sat on the woodblock between us and the house and smoked.

At full-light the crows began to caw in the high pasture and in response to their calling, the hinges of the big oak door trumpeted, and Grandpa emerged. There he stood in stocking feet on the large step-stone in front of the door, boots in one hand, hat and pipe in the other and went through his usual morning routine of "checking the weather."

A tall, spare man with brilliant blue eyes and an explosion of white hair and mustache sitting atop a perpetual frown, he scowled east, then glared west and lastly tested the wind with a licked index finger held high in the air. All eyes followed these mysterious gyrations in rapt expectation. Grandpa let the suspense build as he settled himself on the step-stone and wrestled with his boots. After what seemed an eternity, he dramatically made his one word proclamation, "Hot!"

We all nodded at one another in knowing approval, all except Pap who sat on the woodblock and idly rolled his own.

Water is scarce in the hill country because of the mine drainage and, except for the crick about a hundred yards down from the house, we had no steady supply. Pap wanted a source closer and a bit more reliable, so we'd been digging holes for a month now and had come up totally and completely dry. He wasn't about to give up, mostly because Mom wouldn't let him, so when she suggested Grandpa could find water when no one else could, Pap reluctantly agreed to let him try.

All waited in anticipation while Grandpa sat on the massive, cold stone, laced his boots and buttoned his denim shirt. We hoisted picks, shovels and axes but Grandpa still wasn't ready. He fished a half empty tobacco pouch from somewhere in his trousers and carefully packed his pipe, we chomped at the bit eager to get started, he sat on the step-stone and unhurriedly fiddled with his pipe.

About the time we all relaxed, he suddenly rose and strode to the back of the house and headed straight up towards the orchard, without a word. Pap quickly motioned for us to follow and we grabbed picks, shovels and such and hustled right after them.

What a sight! Grandpa, Pap, my four brothers with the clearing and digging equipment, my sister and me with our knapsacks of sandwiches and water. Trailing Indian fashion, up through the orchard we went, across the ridge above the house, single file all the way. We must have looked like a column of ants from a bird's eye as we crossed and crisscrossed the ridge looking for a likely place to dig a hole.

It never occurred to us to just sit down and let Grandpa do his divining, then come a running. No, no, we were all eager to be there when the site was discovered. So, we panted under our burdens as the old man charged on streaming smoke from that endless pipe like a C&BL locomotive. Across the ridge, down the hill to the crick and back up again we went time after time. Occasionally he would stop and stare trance like as we all caught up to him. Then he would mutter, "Too far, too high, too low, too near the barn," and off we'd go again.

Part Two

The Chosen Spot

As the morning wore on the line began to grow till Pap stopped and gave us his "let's get on with it" look and we quickly closed ranks and pushed on.

About mid-morning I was plodding along, head down, straps of my knapsack digging into my shoulders, sweat stinging my eyes when with a start, I bumped into the brother in front of me. I braced for an elbow shot but he paid no mind which was really unusual. Bending low, I peered under his arm pit to see what the heck was going on. Suddenly, a chill hit me like throwing wide the kitchen door on a freezing, wintry day!

Everyone was standing around Grandpa as he stood in one of his trance-like states again, ramrod straight and rock still, no mutterings this time, however. In a minute, his eyes began to dance, and to different tunes it seemed, cause they were going in opposite directions to one another, and then I realized his head was shaking too. Wilder and wilder the shake became. Like some living thing, it worked its way through his quaking body, intensifying by the second till poor old Grandpa was just a shaking, vibrating, eye popping mess!

All that wild, uncontrollable shaking made his white mane fluff like a sheep in the wind. His eyes were bright and flashing diamond blue and going every which way. The sight of him made me want to run and hide but I knew I wouldn't. I was going to see it through to the end cause, GRANDPA WAS DIVINING!

My brothers and I stared, open mouthed and bug eyed. Sissy fused and Pap picked her up and held her in one arm while he leaned on a shovel with his free hand. Just when you thought it couldn't get any worse, and without so much as moving a boot, Grandpa shook, quivered and vibrated in a full circle one, two, three times, pointed one wildly nervous finger at the ground at his feet and stammered, "DDDIIIGGG HHHEEERRREEE!" Then he made a sound something like, "AAARRRGGGHHH," and collapsed, spread eagled right on the chosen spot!

Holy shamolies! I guess I've seen stranger sights in my life since that day on the mountain but I've never seen anything like the energy and excitement generated by Grandpa's divining performance! He'd hardly hit the ground till my brothers descended on that spot with an aggressiveness to behold.

Pap grabbed Grandpa's limp, rag like form and pulled him to safety as spades, picks, rocks, dirt and war hoops filled the air.

The hole deepened quickly and soon there was only room for two. The rest of us stood around the rim, shouting encouragement, waiting, fighting and arguing for a chance to jump in. Emotion stayed high even through lunch as we ate in shifts and never missed a lick.

I guess having seen Grandpa divine, we knew water was there, just waiting for us to uncover that precious spring. No one was going to miss that, no sir. Every swing of the pick and turn of the shovel brought us closer the treasure we knew was there, just barely out of reach.

We tore through the leaf mold, the black top soil and into the clay like a Hercules Drilling machine. The clay went from blue to yellow to hard pack and we never missed a beat. When the shale appeared, we faltered a minute cause it was too rocky to pick, so we climbed out of the hole for a breather. Pap knew what was coming through and had already been to the barn and back with a heavy mattox, a sledge and a couple of iron bars. The going was tough but I have to tell you in minutes we were back on a torrid pace.

We were about ten feet down now and the shale was too heavy to throw out so we tied a couple of bull ropes to the buckets, hauled them to the top and away. The buckets weighed a ton and my backside burned when sweat ran to where my dungarees rubbed and I prayed for someone to spell me. But you know what, when I looked at Pap down in that hole, stripped to the waist, glistening with sweat as he swung the mattox and pounded the shale to pieces small enough to shovel into the buckets, I felt his energy and determination.

The day was fast getting on when the first trickle of water appeared on the uphill side of the hole. All whooping and hollering had long since turned to quiet resolve and there wasn't any celebration now. Pap and my brother, Big Bill, simply cleaned up the loose shale on the bottom and climbed out.

We all sat around the rim to watch that dry hole magically turn itself into a genuine, pure, mountain water well.

The light was almost gone now as Pap rolled his first smoke in hours, the satisfaction that shone on his face warmed me like a glass of hard cider. We wrapped our gear in an old tarp, stored it in the crotch of a broken maple and headed home.

Part Three

The Rock

Well, I'd love to tell you that by morning the well was over flowing and this story ends here and now with enough cold, sweet, mountain water for all. But, as you have probably guessed, it wasn't over flowing. In fact, it wasn't any better off than the night before, and this story is just picking up.

We hit the spring, that was obvious. The water was flowing beautifully in on the uphill side of the well but, unfortunately, it was going out the downhill side just as fast. The underground spring we uncovered was following an ageless route through the shale straight down the hill, all the way to the crick we guessed.

"Gotta go deeper boys," Pap mused, "She'll never fill this way."

There wasn't much water in the bottom of the well but we bailed it out anyway and wedged a bucket at the mouth of the trickle. Then we began the task of beating on that shale bottom.

Pap and I were at the top taking a breather when I heard Big Bill, shouting that he'd hit a large rock. Pap told him, "Get moving and dig around it!"

Bill hollered back, "Already have and there ain't no edge, least wise not that I can find!"

Pap stood quietly looking down the hill while he finished his water break, then with one cat-like move he was in the bottom of the hole with an iron bar in his hand. He was really agitated as he poked this way and that searching and searching for the edge of that cussed rock. Left, right, uphill, downhill he jammed and poked that bar but, in the end,, he found exactly what Big Bill had found, nothing but rock.

Finally, and at long last, Pap cleaned the loose dirt and shale and called for the sledge.

Now, if you have never seen a strong man work a heavy sledge with skill and dedication, you've missed one of the great joys of life. Pap was not a big man as tall goes but the size of his shoulders and arms made him appear much larger than he was. For as long as I can remember he had thick, wavy, salt and pepper hair and today it was unruly. He was a slight, compact man with handsome features.

We all knew Pap was incredibly strong and smart but that was not his most impressive trait. When he fixed you with those calm, gray eyes, he could warm your heart or freeze it, whatever he desired, and right now he was absolutely glaring at that cussed rock that just seemed to be every- where. This steel coil of a man was preparing to smash that darned rock to smithereens and I just couldn't wait!

Pap readied for action as he removed his shirt and loosened the belt on his trousers. He planted his feet at shoulder width and hefted the sledge. In journeyman fashion, he raised and dropped the sledge in front of him listening for a hollow sound but there was none. So, with no defined starting point he began working methodically on the highest point on the rock. In a minute, a chunk broke off and we all cheered but it proved to be premature.

Pap was getting loose now and in a solid rhythm. The sledge rose and fell, rose and fell with the regularity of an old Prussian march. Sweat covered his back and soaked the rear of his trousers. His chest became pock marked from the little comets that shot from under the sledge and went everywhere. His breathing grew louder and louder in perfect synch with the movement and crash of the sledge. The scene absolutely mesmerized me. Swish, crash, ping, rest. Swish, crash, ping, rest, it was a symphony in the wild and Pap was orchestra, soloist and guest conductor and I was dearly loving it!

The symphony went on and on but the rock held and after a long while the music reached its dramatic climax and began to fade. At long last the "conductor" lowered his baton and stood, calloused hands on hips and sucked wind.

"Bed rock," I heard him mutter between heaves, "Rotten, lousy bedrock."

Part Four

The Arrival

Very early the next morning found us back at the well. Pap wasn't there but he had left word for us boys to get up the hill and cut a hundred saplings and be quick about it. We had no idea why but in good time the saplings were cut, trimmed and stacked neatly about the hole just as we had been told.

The whole bunch of us were just standing around waiting for something to happen. After a while, we got bored and began climbing trees and chunking rocks at one another till someone shouted Pap was coming. We all jumped to attention cause we knew something was about to happen now for sure!

In a minute, I saw him coming up the path. He had a box on his shoulder and there was someone with him. I shinnied up a skinny tree to get a better look and suddenly my heart jumped and skipped a beat or two cause, there following Pap was none other than John Jacob Eubanks!

"Holy cow!" I shouted.

"What, what?" my brothers hollered back.

"Holy cow!" I wailed, "The most interesting and mysterious man on the whole mountain is following Pap and I'm excited!"

Now, John Jacob Eubanks was a man who lived alone in a little, rough cut house high up on the mountain. No one I knew ever got real close to John, he just wasn't that type but he was respected by the local men and kind to the kids.

The women didn't favor John cause, they accused he drank and caroused too much, they insisted that's why he had no wife. Mom was the exception, though, she treated him kindly. Momma said John drank and reveled because he had no wife and that's what made the difference. For his part John treated Mom like she was the queen.

Pap, Mom and John, they all seemed to get along okay. Sometimes Mom would scold him a little but not too much. Like the time John, on a brutally hot summer day, stopped by Grandpa's watering trough on the way home from the mine. He proceeded to take a bath and then walked on home clad in nothing but his work boots and miner's cap with the carbide lantern fastened to the brim. When Mom got after him next day he yes mammed her to death!

As it usually is, the truth about John and his drinking and wild behavior probably was somewhere in the middle. Pap always felt it all had more to do with what he did for a living than anything. John was the only man on the mountain who carried on his special trade, one passed on to him by an elderly gentleman who tragically died in a horrific mining accident. You see, John, was a shot man in the mine.

He was the one, the one who went totally alone into the depths of the dark, damp coal mine with nothing but his courage for company. There, working cautiously by lantern, he'd manually bore holes deep into the coal face. Then he would place dynamite charges into the bored holes to loosen the face. When all was ready, he would survey his work, then detonate the charges, well-hidden some distance away or around a bend.

He would linger awhile to be sure he hadn't loosened the timbers or the face too much and then out he'd come, black from head to toe, even in his mouth, nose and ears. John was somewhat of a hero to the other miners cause, he always turned the mine over to them loose and reasonably safe. And now, here he was, standing, smoking and talking to Pap right at the edge of the well.

At Pap's direction, we hustled and hauled a ladder from the barn since there was absolutely no way John was going to climb bull ropes. In a minute, he was at the bottom of the hole for a better look at the rock. He pulled a stone hammer from the loop on his coveralls and began to test the rock, looking for a flaw.

Pap had us cover part of the hole with the fresh cut saplings and peg them down tight while John continued his search.

After what seemed an eternity John hollered something about trying a mud cap or mud pack charge or something that sounded like that and called for a stick of dynamite. Pap carefully opened the box and picked up a stick wrapped in heavy, red, waxed paper. He got a detonator cord and carried it all over to the rim of the well.

"Just drop it to me," John called and for the first time, Pap hesitated.

"Ned! You not hear me!" shouted John impatiently, "Drop it to me!"

So, Pap held that ugly, red stick directly over him, cut it loose and quickly stepped away from the hole.

Presently, we all emerged from behind the trees and rocks where we were hiding and cautiously crept to the well's edge and peered over. John was busily packing the stick, which he placed directly in the middle of the rock, with hard packed clay. He pushed and prodded that now loaded lump of clay till he had it looking the way he wanted. He grabbed the injected detonator cord protruding from the lump and trailed it up and over the edge as he climbed the ladder.

Once on top, John surveyed his work from the safety of the rim. When he was satisfied he touched the cord to the tip of his cigarette, dropped it and just so casually, watched it go.

I couldn't believe he just stood there and watched that sputtering flame descend to the bottom of the hole and start across the rock face heading directly toward the charge.

"What are you thinking?" I shouted under my breath.

I was about to duck behind my tree again when John casually turned his back to the hole and, KABLOOM, the charge sounded off.

There was a lot of smoke, water and debris in the air but the shot man was already at the bottom of the hole inspecting his handiwork. From the look on his face it was clear that not much had been accomplished. The rock was stubborn and it had held. Now our man felt the challenge and he took to it like a prize hound to the hunt.

And so it went for the rest of the day. John shot charge after charge on that bed rock but it was tough and held fast. By late afternoon all he had to show for his effort was a deep groove down the middle of the rock floor and a lung full of dust.

Part Five

The Solution

My ears were ringing by the time John finally called a halt to the blasting and shouted for Pap to join him in the hole as he fished through his coveralls for a pack of chewing tobacco. He called for a small maple bough and used it as a broom and swept the rock bottom clean. Then, reaching as high as he could, he pulled a piece of soft stone from the clay and used it as a marker as he drew a large X clear across the rock floor.

At the end of each line and where they crossed in the center, he scratched other little X's. In the end, he had five distinct marks scratched onto the rock in very particular places.

The boys, my sister and I lay on our bellies in the cool earth and hung our heads as far into the hole as we dare. We all strained to hear as John explained, "Listen Ned, we need to drill holes in this sun-of-gun at each of the spots I've marked with the stone. Each hole must be just wide enough and deep enough to hold one stick of dynamite."

John grinned at the thought and a little tobacco juice trickled down his chin as he continued, "Do it right, Ned, and we'll split this miserable sucker in to four lovely pieces, promise."

With that and not another word he was up the ladder and gone, to where we could only guess.

Pap wasted no time either as he came up the rope hand over hand and clustered us around the well. He pointed out all the little X's and explained what he wanted us to do.

Sounded pretty simple and easy as he demonstrated with bar and sledge in the soft earth.

"One of you will kneel and hold the drill bar right on the X. Wrap it tightly with burlap to absorb the shock. Your brother will stand over you with the sledge and drive it home."

"Piece a cake," I thought when I got my turn to try. Being the younger on my team I, of course, got to hold the bar. I centered it on the X Pap drew in the dirt and held it steady as Honey Boy pile drived it.

Three swings of the sledge and it was up to the hilt. Nothing to it, we'd have this job done in no time.

Curiously, Pap cautioned us to, "Take your time and work the project this coming week. I gotta go to the mill in town and won't have any free time to help."

I smiled to myself thinking, "We'll knock this baby out and be at the swimming hole in about two shakes of a nanny goat's tail."

Right about then Pap got real serious quiet as he fixed each of us with that unwavering, steady gaze of his and we knew something big was coming.

"Listen up, all of you," Pap said insistently, "No fuss, no muss this week. You holders, hold that drill bar steady and plumb. You strikers, hit square what you aim at, and nothing else. Any accidents on this job and you'll answer to me."

We all nodded and mumbled some inaudible agreement but Pap waved us quiet with one sweep of his arm.

"Here's the rub," he cautioned, "This is where it gets sticky. Just at the moment of impact between drill bar and sledge, blink your eyes. That's right, I said blink your eyes. I don't want anyone ending up with an eye full of shards. Aim the sledge right, hold the bar steady and you'll have no problem. You teams, pair off and practice that for awhile, I'll see you at supper."

And with that, Pap was gone. Well, I'll tell you that was one wrinkle I wasn't prepared for and didn't like. I insisted Honey Boy practice that swing and blink thing a safe distance from me for awhile.

We all fought and argued for some time over swing and blink but Big Bill finally applied a little logic to the situation. He cuffed Honey Boy, Butch and me on the back of the head and we all took notice. Then he graphically described what a chunk of hot rock in the eye would be like and we settled down and practiced in earnest after that.

We eventually realized the only thing worse than hot rock in the eye would be Pap when he found out we hadn't followed his orders and he had to explain it all to Mom.

Part Six

The Assault

There is absolutely nothing in this world more beautiful that an early summer sunrise in the hill country. Those first slanting rays coming through the trees are truly magical. As the rays grow shorter and the light improves it's as if the country side is reborn, all in for another day.

This Monday morning was more than special because today marked the beginning of the end of that lousy, rotten bed rock that stood between us and enough cool, fresh mountain water to revel in. Today was the day and we just couldn't wait to get started.

"C'mon guys," shouted Butch, "By late afternoon we'll be lounging in the calm water of Billy's Dam or playing in the rapids below. Whatever, this job will be done and the smell of fresh water will be sweet!"

The air was cool and clean and Honey Boy and I were so eager, we volunteered to start it off. In the bottom of the pit I knelt on the rock, wrapped the burlap tightly around the drill bar and carefully placed the tip in the center of the lower left X. For the third time, I checked my plumb and finally nodded to Honey Boy to smash it home.

What happened next is really hard to explain. I have never in my life been struck by lightning but, believe you me if I ever am I'll know exactly how it will feel.

When the head of the slightly errant sledge met the top of the not-so-plumb drill bar the results were disastrous! The bar shot from my hands and glanced off my chin as the head of the sledge grazed my shoulder and ribs and a thousand explosions went off within me! The worst was, however, it all happened so fast, so terribly fast! There was no time to react!

As I came to my senses Big Bill was beside me cradling my head in the crook of his arm and slapping my face urgently with water. Honey Boy caught most of the blame cause he was older and "should've known better" but I got my share of it as well. Bill grinned when it looked like we were both bruised but okay and, after all, we had remembered to blink.

Honey Boy and I were ejected from the work site as team number two took over the effort. Bill banished us to a practice spot a long way from the well.

It was embarrassing but believe you me practice we did! Neither of us wanted a repeat of our miserable performance and besides, what would Pap say when he found out.

Everything about me was hurting but I wasn't about to complain for fear of ridicule, so I toughed it out and grinned, as best I could. When we got our chance to get back on the job and surveyed the little progress made by team number two, it was enough to give you heartburn. With a general sinking feeling we all realized what Pap meant when he told us to "work the project this week." That miserable rock was stubborn and would not yield easily.

It may sound strange but I felt a kind of admiration for its strength and toughness. It had a permanent quality about it that you couldn't ignore. That kind feeling evaporated quickly, however, when back on the assault with bar and sledge.

Part Seven

Drill and Drill Some More

Needless to say, we never made it to Billy's Dam that week but we did get the holes pretty much done, or so we thought. Toward the end of the week Pap was still nowhere to be seen.

Mom gave us the tough news, "Things have gone badly at the mill, boys, we may not see your Pap for awhile. He sent word for you to continue with your drilling."

We loudly protested we thought the holes were done but Mom stated with finality, "If your Pap says work on your drilling, then you'd best work on your drilling."

And, as they say, that was that!

The only way to catch Pap when the mill was running rough was very early in the morning or very late at night. Big Bill tried over the weekend and reported back that Pap was in no mood to talk and argue. So, Monday morning found us back at the well and hard at it.

We got after Bill to try again but he shouted, "I don't care how deep the darn holes get to, I'm not about to face up to Pap again, not any time soon anyway!"

Towards the end of the second week of drilling, one sorrowful morning we were, the whole gang of us, sitting around the hole with our feet dangling over the edge and just staring into the pit. There was gloom in the air for sure cause we were so worn out on this job with blistered hands and aching muscles, we just didn't know what to do next. My sister, Sal, had lanced and dressed so many blisters and rubbed so much liniment she was ready to throw in the towel.

Almost as one we noticed something different in the air. The whole bunch of us immediately perked up as the sweet- smelling odor of Grandpa's Rum and Maple pipe tobacco caught us all by surprise. We knew he was coming long before he stepped lightly through the trees. He had to be in a good mood cause that's when he broke out the Rum and Maple instead of that old rough smelling Cuttey Pipe he usually burned.

The old man was very tall and this morning he looked the part as he stood before us poker straight from the top of his big, broad brimmed hat to the toes of his boots. As usual, he said nothing but he must have felt our gloom and doom, it was pretty hard to miss. Leaning gently on his prized cherry walking stick, he stood there quietly puffing on that glowing pipe and fixed one questioning eye on Big Bill.

"Look Grandpa, looky here," Bill stammered, "We think the holes are plenty done but Pap and John are nowhere to be seen and all we have are orders to drill. And believe me Grandpa, without Pap's okay we are gonna drill clear to China or until John or Pap shows up, whichever comes first cause if Pap says drill, you drill!

Part Eight

The Rescue

Grandpa slowly and impressively walked round and round the well peering intently from all sides. We knew the wheels were turning cause he had that look in his eye. Then, suddenly a little corner smile showed under that white, bushy mustache. We were sure he had some kind of solution for us but none dreamed what was really going on under that big hat.

Ever the gentleman, he dramatically removed his Outback leather hat and gave it a careful inspection as the tension built. He pridefully hung it securely on a broken willow branch and turned to face the pit. Now remember, Grandpa never said much, that was just his way. You had to kind of follow along to know what he was up to but when he climbed down into the well we still hadn't figured it.

At the bottom of the well Grandpa slowly lowered himself to the rock floor and inspected our handiwork for awhile. At long last, he looked up at Big Bill and pointed to the dynamite box. He still hadn't said a word, he just sat there, arm outstretched, index finger pointing to the box labeled, "EXTREME DANGER—CONTENTS ARE EXPLOSIVE."

Poor Bill, he was dumbfounded and didn't know what in the world to do so he pleaded, "Maybe, just maybe, we should wait for John."

The old man's demeanor changed in a split second. He glared back at Bill and spoke his first words of the day, "I was blasting stumps when John was still a snot nose! Now pass that darned box or I'll come up and get it myself and give you a good kicken besides!"

Well, what could we do? We tied a rope to each of the box end handles and gently lowered it to the rock floor. Grandpa opened the box and casually removed five of the ugly red sticks. Grabbing one by the very end he inserted the first stick as far into the hole as his fingers would allow, then he turned it loose. It made a soft little plop when it hit bottom. He slid around the rock floor on his backside and gently repeated the process four more times and called for the detonator cord.

So far the operation had gone smoothly but now Grandpa stalled. As he tried to insert the fuse into the top end of the explosive, he realized he couldn't properly reach it! The stick in fact was sufficiently and completely out of reach!

Perplexed, Grandpa leaned back against the clay wall, pulled his knees to his chest, clasp his hands around them, and there he sat and sat and sat.

In utter astonishment, we all pulled away from the hole whispering in frantic, low tones, "What's he doing? What's he going to do now? What should we do? What will Pap and John say? Is Grandpa going to blow himself to smithereens? Someone go get Grandma! Lordy, lordy, what's going to happen now?"

We were quickly drawn back to the well when the familiar smell of pipe tobacco tickled noses again. I peered over the edge and there he sat, knees drawn up, puffing on that infernal pipe. Man oh man, that may or may not be good thing!

It was so quiet it made my ears ring if you could imagine such a thing. I could even hear the rattle of the cow's bells as they foraged through distant pastures. The tension hung like an evening fog, growing thicker and thicker by the minute.

What to do? I had no earthly idea. So, I did the only thing I knew to do, I looked to my dear brother Big Bill for an answer. Low and forever behold, there he stood, ramrod straight, hands clasped securely in front of him, head tilted back, staring through the canopy overhead and at the heavens beyond, or so I guessed, lips moving curiously.

And so, I put my trust completely in my wonderful, big brother and did the same. Pretty soon we were all emulating Bill and there we stood, the whole gang of us. Imagine if you can the bunch of us, encircling that well in quiet solitude, hands clasped securely in front, heads tilted back, serene look on our faces. What a pious sight we must have been.

Meanwhile as Grandpa sat in the bottom of the well puffing, thinking and musing, and we stood face up in quiet supplication, it was right at that very moment that we witnessed a singular occurrence the likes of which we had never before seen nor even imagined.

Part Nine

The Little Miracle

High in the very top of an ancient broad leaf oak tree, a single skinny piece of branch reached the end of its life and gave itself to the whims of a slight breeze. The slender, little stick tumbled and twirled as it gently fell down, down, down right into the well where Grandpa sat and, straight as an arrow, lodged itself directly into the first charged hole at his feet.

Good gosh amighty! Fancy that if you can!

Grandpa seemed bemused and a little addled by it all. He cocked his head one way then the other as he peered intently at his little visitor. Was there meaning in this unusual happening? Gramps sure felt that there was cause he couldn't divert his eyes from his little friend. He stared and stared and studied and studied until at long last he gingerly reached out and grasped the top end of the little omen just barely protruding from the charged hole. Trancelike, he withdrew the stick and held it directly in front of him.

As Grandpa mentally gauged the length, breadth and worth of the tiny piece of branch his normally brilliant blue eyes suddenly became nova-like. I did not know exactly what revelation flashed through him but it was very obvious and dramatic, just like his divining.

With a grin growing by the second, he carefully extracted a stick of dynamite from the box, placing the branch and the explosive side by side on the rock floor. His eyes were absolutely dancing with excitement now as a solution to his dilemma began to dawn.

"This must be it," I thought, but was instantly taken aback at Grandpa's next move. Without a word but with the broadest smile protruding from under that white, bushy mustache he pulled four more sticks of the ugly red explosive from the box. In workman like fashion he lowered a stick into each hole with the very top just about even with the rock floor.

My mind raced at break neck speed, "What the heck is he doing, he double charged every hole! John never double charged one! Holy cow what is he doing? Where is John and Pap? Bill, Bill what should we do?"

We were in a tiz with excitement laced with fear but Bill calmly continued to do the only thing he knew to do as he stood rock still, staring at the heavens, lips mysteriously moving ever so slightly but ever so quickly.

Meanwhile, Grandpa, oblivious to our fear and trepidation, quickly went on with his self- appointed task. Inserting a detonator cord in each top stick he evened their length, gathered them to the middle of the well and twisted them together. Attaching a single cord to the twisted pack, he carefully played it over the rock floor to the ladder then up and out of the well.

As my dear Grandpa emerged from the well trailing that fateful cord behind him, eyes flashing, beaming with confidence, humming a few bars of Glory Hallelujah through pursed lips, I tell you he looked absolutely messianic! He was about to solve this miserable rock problem completely, on his own, and he was just bursting with himself. He had chosen this spot through his divining and by golly he would see it through to a joyful, victorious end. His old denim shirt rose and fell in rhythm with his rapid breathing and racing heart. What a sight he was! Gosh, that image is embedded in my mind to this very day as much because of what he had done up to this point, and what was about to happen next!

"Grandpa, Grandpa what about the rest of the dynamite?" Bill shouted frantically.

Grandpa ignored Bill's distraught cry as, grunting impatiently, he waved us all to a safe distance from the well. Limping along, he trailed the cord to and over the huge pile of rocks, dirt and shale extracted from the well. He flopped down behind the protective pile of debris and, without hesitation, jammed the end of the detonator cord into the bowl of his pipe and began to puff! Lord have mercy on us all!

Little did my Grandpa know or even suspect that he was about to become an instrument of change never before seen on the mountain.

One could not document the many life altering experiences which occurred that day as a result of his actions.

The most dramatic effect was of course upon Grandpa himself. There were others though, so many others who in an instant went through an enlightening process that would last forever and a day.

Part Ten

Mr. Shabarra

Well beyond the cabbage field at the back of our place our nearest neighbors lived on a small, hillside farm fenced and terraced in old world tradition. Immigrants from somewhere in eastern Europe the Shabarra's knew how to get the most from their little farm.

They were friendly enough when we met in the field, at the crick or on the path to town. Although Mr. and Mrs. Never learned much English we all got along with a lot of gesturing and grinning at one another and it worked out okay, I guess.

When Mr. Shabarra was feeling good he tried to share all kinds of secrets like how to grow onions year to year without planting, or how to hunt and pick mushrooms that wouldn't kill you.

Mrs. Shabarra was always offering us some of her favorite specialties like sautéed giant sunflower seeds or fresh baked paguch.

In his later years the elderly gentleman had grown somewhat weary of the confining life on the little farm. Nostalgically, he longed for the excitement of the political unrest always prevalent in his native land. His younger brother, still living in the old country, wrote frequently describing his latest escapades of do and daring. It was the bright spot in the old man's day and he immersed himself in the telling and lived impatiently for the next installment.

On the morning of that direful day the door to the little country cottage creaked open and Mr. Shabarra stood, dressed only in trousers and long handle top, shuffling his feet in the thin morning sunlight. Framed in the kitchen doorway, he tested the nip in the chilly air.

A wizened little man with a natural squint, he sucked air noisily through a near toothless mouth. His normally pained expression was heightened by the anticipation of a bare foot dash down the long stone walk, still cold and damp with morning dew, to the relative privacy and safety of the outhouse. He almost resolved not to go till he spied Mrs. Shabarra watching him intently from the other side of the garden. He quickly realized it was down the walk to the outhouse or up the path to the garden, badly in need of weeding. The outhouse won out. So, armed with a month-old newspaper and his brother's latest letter, he laid his head back and set out at top speed, bony knees and elbows pumping, for his private sanctuary.

Mrs. Shabarra stood knee deep in onions and watched him go. A big, square woman full of rolls and folds she bit down on her pipe and grinned at the sight. Somewhere inside the ample petticoats and aprons a low chuckle began as she recalled the time the old man had on just such an occasion, stumped his toe on the uneven walk and went wind milling and screaming, right past the outhouse, over the rail and into the pig sty! No such luck today, however, as the bang and rattle of door and latch heralded a safe arrival. The old woman adjusted her sun bonnet and bent to her onions and the low rumbling chuckle continued for some time.

Mr. Shabarra sat on the left side of the two holer, bent double, chest on knees, rubbing the circulation back into his aching feet. Still wheezing from his run, he mumbled threats at the stone cold walk and at his wife's continuing chuckle.

He quickly scanned the old newspaper and turned to his brother's letter, both full of the same news. The civil distress in his native land was happily approaching disaster. A group of dissidents had confiscated the ceremonial cannon from the town square and laid siege to the dictator's palace. Apparently, he had incurred public disfavor with a decree against frivolous night revelry.

So, lost in thought, the old man shifted slightly to catch the light streaming through the crescent at the top of the door and, longingly, read on.

Part Eleven

Preacher Lydic

Down the mountain near the river it was already getting warm and muggy. Bible School was nearly over for this morning and everyone was glad.

The children were especially happy cause this was the last class of the week. No more swatting at flies that crept through the crack in the door and buzzed around sweaty little heads. No more trying to color pictures of Jesus while the paper stuck to your forearm and the crayons went limp in your hand. No more embarrassment at finding out after turning the smudgy picture in that it is doubtful Jesus was a blue-eyed blond anyway. But, most of all, no more Preacher Lydic.

Miss Wainwright collected the smudgy pictures cheerfully. She was especially happy cause this was the last class of the week and the weekend was full of promise. Ah, this will be a weekend full of fun, welcome and deserved. There is the Mountain Charity Box Social tonight on the square where her beau is sure to bid an outrageous sum for the privilege of sharing a basket of crispy fried chicken lovingly prepared by her own hand.

"Ah yes, the weekend is full of promise," she thought as she boxed the last of the slippery, limp crayons, "And best of all, no more Preacher Lydic."

The "good" preacher sat in the last pew well away from his perspiring charges. He polished his spectacles for the third time, the better to watch Miss Wainwright, and set them atop a bulbous nose.

As he sat and stared, open mouthed, drooling slightly, he slicked back his too long hair and worked at straightening his rumpled black suit. The muggy air conspired with his portly frame and thoroughly sabotaged his efforts till, with a silent cry of frustration, he gave up in despair.

At the front of the sanctuary Miss Wainwright straightened from her task and the preacher quickly turned his hot and magnified gaze from her to the imitation, stained glass window behind and above her. The image on the window was that of Jesus of Nazareth. The scene was a plush, green country side with a red robed Jesus walking toward the viewer, arms outstretched, welcoming, beseeching. Poor workmanship and the passage of time had, however, rendered the features and details quite indistinct.

Now, in the preacher's high state of self- induced excitement, his mind's eye suddenly saw Jesus glaring at him, reaching for him! He blinked several times then closed his eyes tightly to block out the image.

"Mind me Justin Lydic," his wife had warned him when she first discovered his philandering nature, "Jesus will not let you lead a sinful life. You're a man of the cloth and you must not defile your office! Jesus will not let you! Jesus will not let you! Jesus will get you!"

"JESUS- K- RIST!" the preacher shouted as his eyes flew open and he bolted to his feet!

Suddenly conscious that every eye in the church was on him, he summoned his most benevolent and practiced preacher's smile and slowly walked to the front of the sanctuary.

"Jesus Christ," he said in his smooth preacher's voice, "The ever presence of Jesus Christ will keep the devil at bay. Class dismissed."

A slight breeze came through the open door for but a second and the children were gone. The preacher stared at the door till he could no longer hear the happy little voices but only the buzz of a bumble bee that had flown in as the children had flown out.

The "good man" turned slowly to Miss Wainwright who, with her back to him, was susceptibly bent over packing bible story books into a large carrying case. He simply made no effort to stifle a most lecherous grin twitching at the left corner of his mouth.

"A preacher I am," he said to himself, "But today ain't Sunday!"

Part Twelve

Prelude to Disaster

And so, it would seem that a time was fixed on that beautiful, calm summer morning as surely as the stars are fixed in the heavens. The most dramatic and significant emotional experience in the lives many of the inhabitants of the rustic mountain community of Tanneryville was about to unfold.

In years to come most who witnessed the day would recall and tell their own, private version of the events and repercussions that ensued.

The relentless passage of time will dim vision and weaken knees but nothing has or ever will alter the memory of the cataclysmic series of events that were about to evolve.

Part Thirteen

The Finale

As Grandpa sat puffing on his pipe, the detonator cord jammed into the now glowing bowl suddenly burst into life scorching the old man's eyebrows and mustache.

"Ow, ow, ow," he bawled as he yanked the cord from his pipe and quickly threw it to the ground where it hissed and spit and danced up and over the pile of rubble and headed toward the well.

The whole gang of us were hugging the ground behind the protective mound, waiting for the disaster we knew was sure to come.

In a minute, it got the best of me and I nervously crawled to the top of the heap and peered over. That angry little flame continued its reel across no man's land towards the rim of the well.

"Stop, stop!" I shouted but without a second of hesitation or fanfare, it went over the edge and disappeared, just like that!

With that ugly, little dancer now out of sight there was nothing to see so I hunkered down behind the barricade, kissed the dirt and waited. Desperately I tried to track the flame's progress by the echo of the pop, hiss and crackle as it descended to the rock floor and proceeded on its date with destiny.

The tension was electric and the waiting interminable and I gasped as I realized I hadn't been breathing for some time.

Oddly enough, in the midst of it all a surreal calmness ensued but when the hissing and sputtering and crackling stopped we all knew disaster was imminent. Suddenly and totally without warning, Grandpa bolted to his feet, clambered to the top of the barricade, arms stretched skyward, pointed his walking stick to the heavens and bellowed, "FIRE IN THE HOOOOLE!"

KAAAAAABLOOOOOOM!

The blast was immediate, fierce and deafening as a wall of flame the height of Rager Mountain shot from the pit! The protective covering of saplings, so carefully cut, placed and pegged went right along with it! The shock wave hit the pile of debris we cowered behind and pelted us with hot, dirty water and rocks!

But the worst of it all, the very worst of it all was, Grandpa was simply gone! He totally vanished from view! One second he was standing heroically on top of the mound just above me, looking all the world like Moses at the Red Sea and the next, he was gone! I could not breathe nor comprehend what had just happened. I wet my pants and didn't care. My dear Grandpa was really and truly gone!

My mind reeled as I tried to think, to reason, but the ringing in my head wouldn't allow it. Frantically, I scrambled to the top of the mound and that's when I heard it: oooole, oooole, oooole, oooole!

It was Grandpa! His voice rebounded from the rocks and trees as, propelled by the blast, he tumbled, head over heels backward down the hill! Each time he rolled over and his head popped up, like an angry puppet, blue eyes burning, white hair and mustache singed and bristling, out would come another, "Oooole!"

And so he went on down the hill with each, "Oooole!" getting fainter and fainter until at last he came to rest beneath the old, moss covered watering trough that sat prominently on the bank alongside the crick.

Grandpa's watering trough had been hewn from a single gigantic pine log and had been used by man and beast alike ever since. We never did know who really made the trough since Grandpa's story varied according to his mood. Our nameless worker spent many an hour burning and chiseling the innards out of that huge tree then dragging, rolling and manhandling that rascal into the perfect position.

 He set it where the crick dropped a few feet, then made a little crook around. There, propped up on two boulders, with the wooden sluice feeding in one end, and the overflow at the other, she stood and stood and stood. The wood swelled and grew green, the rocks sunk into the soft crick bank and she became a permanent fixture in the hollow.

Horses drank, Grandpa washed, strangers met, kids swam, love won, grapes grew and the dusty county road edged closer and closer to Grandpa's watering trough in the hollow.

All those years of service to friend and stranger, man and beast, tame and wild had taken their toll on that stately pine but still she was about to perform a feat that would forever crown her career.

As my beloved Grandpa lay beneath her, inert, eyes wide and fixed, blinking in rhythm with the water dripping on his head, an occasional weak and muted, "Oooole," coming forth, in regal style, she performed her final act.

With the rush of a hundred freight trains and a crash louder than the explosion itself, a ton of screaming, scorching rock, mud and debris thundered down and around the trough literally splitting it in two, dumping its frigid contents on Grandpa! The old man lay face up in the muck and moss, surrounded by smoking rocks and mud, battered but alive murmuring, "Oooole, oooole, oooole!"

Part Fourteen

The Conversion

Across the way Mr. Shabarra sat, stone still on the left side of the two holer, lost in thought, deep into his brother's letter about the siege of the dictator's palace.

For a moment, he thought he actually heard the canon blast and that shook him a little. When the small stones began to pelt the outhouse, he was sure he heard rifle fire so engrossed was he. Suddenly, a cannon ball in the guise of a large rock struck the wall up near the eave. The wood splintered showering him with "shrapnel" and the poor man became shell shocked!

The panicked "soldier" burst from the outhouse trying to run and pull up his pants at the same time! As fast as fast could be, he fled to the relative safety of the garden and his wife's ample skirts and petticoats.

Mrs. Shabarra was both shocked and amused as she bent double, lifted her skirts and found herself upside down and eye ball to eye ball with her husband. Since she was stone deaf and hadn't heard a peep of the blast, she had no idea that her husband was hiding from the "enemy."

"Heh, heh, heh," giggled the "Old soldier" as he nervously grinned at his "Protector." Then, still on all fours and trailing his britches behind him, he began weeding as he had never weeded before. Thoughts of the glorious uprising in the old country banished forever from his mind.

Mrs. Shabarra, still unaware of the circumstances, dumped the contents of her picking bucket, turned it bottom up and sat. For the first time in a coon's age she grinned, puffed gently on her pipe and watched the old man go!

Part Fifteen

The Comeuppance

In the little church, down by the river, Miss Wainwright was still bent over cheerfully packing bible story books into a carrying case, her back turned to Preacher Lydic. When the sound of the explosion reached there, she quickly straightened and looked in the direction of the disturbance, unaware that the blast had stayed the "good" preacher's hand just inches from her. The concussion wave rattled the doors and windows, particularly the imitation, stained glass window at the top front of the sanctuary.

The preacher, hand still outstretched, stood in confusion and stared at the image of Jesus which ominously seemed to be moving. A large rock fragment broke the spell as it struck the base of the outside wall. The resulting vibration shook the window completely loose and our red robed Jesus, arms outstretched and reaching, went airborne hovering directly over the preacher's head as his wife's prediction exploded in his head, "JESUS WILL GET YOU!"

"AIIIEEEEE," Preacher Lydic screamed as he hit the door on the dead run, knocking it completely off its hinges, tore out in the direction of the river where the railroad tracks followed by.

As luck would have it a slow- moving freight was just beginning to pick up steam having negotiated a tough curve in the tracks. The last anyone ever saw of Preacher Lydic was a black suited man, hair and coat tail flying, desperately trying to cling to the very last car of a rapidly accelerating freight train headed to somewhere in the wilds of West Virginia.

Regardless of the circumstances, the men of the community breathed a little easier knowing the preacher was long gone from the area.

On an upbeat, Mrs. Lydic took over the running of the church and since she was more interested in socializing than sermonizing, it fared rather well.

Afterword

The echo of the blast faded and the dust blew over the mountain, but tension remained very high among the populace for some time. It took awhile for the folk to realize it was really over. The mushroom that welled up from the blast carried rocks and debris quite a distance. Fortunately, aside from Grandpa, his watering trough and the church, no real damage occurred and no one else was harmed, not physically at least.

Preacher Lydic was gone which didn't hurt anyone's feelings, besides, everyone liked Mrs. Lydic anyway, especially the men.

The church was eventually restored but the imitation, stained glass window was a memory. You could almost believe that our red robed Jesus performed his saving task and moved on to another, friendlier dimension.

The first item of interest however, was Grandpa's watering trough. The travelers along the county road just couldn't get by without that relic, so they had it replaced. Lacking history of course, it would never be the same but it would have to do.

My Grandpa was a long while on the mend. He gradually recovered from the experience and regained his old swagger. He forever swore off searching for water though.

"I will divine no more," is the way he put it.

Talk of divining leads us right back to the very beginning. It would be great to be able to say that in the end it was all worth-while. John showed up and inspected the rock and determined the heavy charge had done considerable damage to our old foe. Sadly, the severe concussion had also diverted the underground stream to heaven only knows where. The well was bone dry.

Over time people took it all in stride. The telling and retelling enhanced the story until it became another colorful chapter in the fascinating, legendary history of Tanneryville.

They're really good people these hill folk, tough too. I think the general mood amongst them could best be summed up in the words of Mrs. Emma Jean Sturbutzle, a coal miner's widow who lived near the foot of the hill. She was up on a step ladder picking rocks and stones from her porch roof when a passer- by asked for her thoughts. Ms. Emma paused, brushed a lock of hair from her face and replied,

"Well, people gotta have water, don't they?"

MISTER PHIKIT'S BRUNCH

An Easter Story

What are human's that You are mindful of them, mere mortals that You care for them? Yet You have made them little less than a God, crowned them with glory and honor.

-    Psalm Eight

MISTER PHIKIT'S BRUNCH

Part One

The young girl nimbly stepped up on the front bumper of the freightliner. Gathering her long, dark hair in one hand and pulling it aside, she stood on tip toe, thrust her head under the hood of the rig and shouted, "Hey! Mr. Phiket! Whatcha doin down there?"

The older gentlemen, lying on his back, shifted his creeper slightly that he could see up at Marty Pam's smiling face framed within the myriad wires, rods and working parts of the engine above him.

"I'm tightening the motor mounts on this engine, what's it look like anyway missey!" Mister Phikit called back.

"Hey, you sure you know what you're doin?" Marty replied.

And with that, they both snickered for a moment and then erupted in laughter. You see, that exchange was a favorite little game the two friends never tired of playing. And play they did, now and then and every chance they got.

The episode though fresh in mind, took them back, way back to their very first meeting which occurred some years ago now:

It was about the time that the Great Traveling Circus, the greatest show on earth, chose the Madison County fairgrounds as their winter quarters. Here in the relative quiet of the country side they determined to practice the three R's of the circus: Rest, repair and rehearse. It just so happened the gentleman's little homestead bordered the fairground on the far back side. Now, this Mister Phikit was a unique man, indeed. The locals knew him by his surname of course, but his reputation was such that he was known far and wide, throughout the county simply as: Mister Fixit.

There just wasn't a single, solitary piece of machinery or equipment around that he could not repair and in fact, make run smoother, longer and better. His talent though obvious was difficult to describe. For lack of a better term, let's just say he was blessed with true, mechanical insight.

One particularly mild, winter day Mr. Pam, the ring master from the circus, came to the little machine shop located directly behind Mister Fixit's house. He lingered in the weak but pleasant sunshine long enough to read the sign above the door, "WELCOME TO MR. FIXIT'S WORLD, COME ON IN." "This is my man," he thought as he entered the shop. The two men had barely exchanged a greeting before Mr. Pam urgently asked the gentleman to come to the fair grounds to do some very necessary work for them. Spring was quickly approaching and they desperately needed to prepare for the upcoming, heavy traveling season. With a smile, the gentleman unconsciously brushed back his mustache as he readily nodded in agreement of course, because after all he was Mister Fixit, that's what he did.

Once over at the fair -grounds our man was hard at it, working diligently and nonstop as was his custom when little Marty Pam, the ringmaster's daughter, came skipping round. She abruptly stopped and stood so close behind she was nearly on his very heels. The little lady stared up at him for a long while, frowning in concentration. Finally, she took a deep breath, cupped her hands around her mouth to form a little bugle and hollered, "Hey! What's your name Mifter and what are you doin there?"

Startled and agitated at the intrusion, the gentleman quickly jerked half around and brusquely shouted back, "People call me Mister Fixit and I'm working on this boiler, what's it look like anyway missey!"

Now, little Marty Pam was in the process of growing some new front teeth. She was close and hard at it but hadn't gotten there quite yet so when she tried to pronounce his name well, it just didn't come out right, infact, not right at all.

"Hey, Mifter Phikit, you sure you know what you're doin?" she belted out.

The gentlemen, nailed totally unawares, was speechless so he put his wrench down and stared long and hard at the little girl. The sight, however, of this curly headed, gap toothed moppet with her bony legs sticking out from under a short skirt, standing there scowling up at him, warmed his heart and his demeanor quickly softened.

"Tell you what," he finally replied unable to hide the half grin at the corner of his mouth, "You can call me Mister Phikit and I'll call you Little Miss Smarty Pants! Now then, how's that?"

And as the old poet said, that was that. The clever notion took root and to the very day the two are known all across the fair grounds and beyond as Mister Phikit and Smarty Pants. Their common joke really helped to solidify their friendship and they willingly followed the routine at every opportunity, laughing all the while as all who listened smiled.

Part Two

Now, we pick up our story on a spring like Thursday afternoon before Good Friday when Smarty Pants asked Mister Phikit, "Hey, whatcha doin over Easter weekend Mister Phikit?"

"Well," the gentlemen replied with a touch of sadness in his voice, "We usually have big doins and a great Easter Brunch. But with the kids all grown and the least now gone out the door, I guess the Missus and I will just have a quiet time. Maybe we'll take a walk if the weather's nice, or read a book if it isn't, or maybe I'll just fix something, I don't know."

Suddenly the gentlemen's eyes brightened and he perked up as he said, "Say, say Smarty Pants I have great idea! Why don't you come on over and enjoy an Easter Brunch with us? The Missus is a fabulously good cook and since she can't get used to cooking for two, we always have way more than we could ever need."

"Wow, wow, wow, what a super, neato, keen idea!" shouted Smarty excitedly. "But, say, say Mister Phikit, I almost forgot," she continued in a more subdued tone, "I already promised to have brunch with some of my friends here at the circus commissary."

"Won't be the same for sure but probably wouldn't be right to disappoint them either." She paused and kinda scrunched up her face as she explained, "You know sir, some of my friends, they just don't have any place to go, if you know what I mean."

"Well, well," the gentleman quickly and eagerly replied, becoming more excited by the prospect, "Why don't you just bring a few of your friends with you?"

"Good gosh amighty, you mean it Mister Phikit! You wouldn't mind! Missus Phikit wouldn't mind!" Smarty Pants shouted excitedly. "Oh wow, wow, wow, wait till I tell my friends!" she called over her shoulder as she dashed across the fairway on a clear and urgent mission.

Part Three

The time is now ten o'clock Easter Sunday morning and Mister and Missus Phikit, already home from their sunrise service, are busily preparing. The odd sound of a truck bumping and rattling down the rocky lane to their house broke the silence and got Mister Phikit's attention. He walked to the front window and when he pulled the curtain aside the scene looked very familiar and immediately he thought he recognized the approaching vehicle. With a roar and a rush, the big semi rolled right up into his front yard and turned slightly to the left. The name emblazoned on the side of the door read, "The Great Traveling Circus."

"Say, that's the very truck I worked on the other day," he thought as he opened the front door and stood on the sill staring, somewhat confused. The engine shut down and a long, quiet pause ensued as the dust settled.

Suddenly, with a screech and a bang the passenger door on the cab burst open and little Miss Smarty Pants, decked in Easter finery, jumped cleanly from the truck to the ground! As fast as fast could be, with hair, ribbons and skirts a flying, she ran across the yard and bounded up the porch steps two and three at a time.

"Please don't be upset with me Mister Phikit," she breathlessly began, "But when word got around the fairway that you invited some of us to brunch, suddenly everybody thought this meant them and they really, really wanted to come too and I just couldn't say no! Remember, sir, when I told you that some of my friends just didn't have any place to go? Well, the whole, honest-to-goodness truth of it all is, they just don't get many invitations! Don't worry about food, everybody brought something with them, even if it is from the commissary. They are all just absolutely overjoyed to actually be invited to your famously, wonderful Easter brunch. Please say it's okay Mister Phikit, please!"

As Smarty Pants desperately pleaded with Mister Phikit, the gentleman continued to stare as people by the dozens began piling from the vehicle. From the cab came the driver Atlas the strong man, then from the trailer came Al the albino, followed by Barby the bearded lady, Skye the world's tallest man, Humongo the fat lady,

Chita the monkey boy, Gastro the geek, Twisto the contorted, Lupus the wolfman, Bones the human skeleton, Awfulla the world's ugliest woman, Pic the tattooed man, Stumpy Joe and his midget wrestlers and on and on and on they came until every freak and geek imaginable, all of the exotic, fascinating, shocking people who make the great circus sideshow what it is, stood in Mister Phikit's front yard!

The poor man stood jaw dropped and wide eyed, unsure what to do or even to think. He tried to mouthe the word, "Welcome," but it just wouldn't come. And then, Missus Phikit, who had heard all the commotion and had come to see, quietly came up behind her husband and gently pushed by. Firmly, she took his hand in hers and, together, they walked to the front edge of the porch. Mister Phikit struggled to follow his wife's lead as in near unison, they raised their outstretched arms and cried,

"WELCOME, ALL OF YOU, FRIENDS OF SMARTY! WELCOME TO PHIKIT' S EASTER BRUNCH!"

And with that, a cheer rose up from the crowd that was probably heard half way to Memphis! And then by golly, something miraculous happened. In true circus-like fashion the yard exploded in activity! From out of the semi came a huge tent, folding tables and chairs. A portable broiler and grill the truck had in tow were wheeled into position and before you could say, "Holy Shamolies," the Phikit's front yard was transformed into a banquet arena!

But it didn't stop there, cause in two shakes of a nanny goat's tail, the table was set and the food was warming. The laughter, noise and excitement were outrageous as everyone bumped and crowded around anxious for the festivities to begin.

Part Four

A bearded, elfish little man, name of Mister Goodspeak, climbed the rungs of his chair and stood upon the seat. He picked up a glass and spoon and, holding the bottom of the glass in the palm of his hand, he began to gently tap the glass with the spoon. A high-pitched tinkle, tinkle, tinkle soon quieted the raucous crowd and they all looked to their friend in anticipation.

Mister Goodspeak stood on his chair, hands neatly at his sides, ram rod straight. He removed his ever, present green derby revealing a tousle of salt and pepper hair and thrust his chin so far forward that his beard stood straight out.

"I would like to say a few words if you don't mind," he announced in a clear and pleasant baritone that belied his diminutive appearance.

"Okay, okay but make it quick!" Stumpy Joe called back.

"Yeah quick," hollered Atlas, "Real, real quick. I'm hungry as a horse!"

The crowd, enjoying the levity, roared in laughter but quieted quickly in deference to their respected elder. Completely unperturbed, Mister Goodspeak calmly looked over the gathering, comfortably and warmly digesting the scene in front of him and when the time was right, he began to speak:

"We bill our Great Traveling Circus as the greatest show on earth and actually, we are pretty good. But in truth, my friends, we are not even close!" The crowd of circus people smiled and settled in for they all knew and loved their learned friend and was more than anxious to hear those "few words" he wanted to say. You see, Mister Goodspeak always framed his lectures in a way they could relate to and in words they could easily understand. An atmosphere of eagerness pervaded the air as the gentleman continued,

"The Greatest Show on Earth in actuality began over two thousand years ago. Originally set and staged in a small, obscure Roman Province in the middle east. It has since spread around the world and is running SRO to this very day! This, my friends, was an extraordinarily impressive three ring extravaganza with an outstanding local headliner from the hill country performing in the center ring."

"Now, my dears, let it be known that this headliner who went by the name of Jesus, was the absolute star of the show. No ordinary performer mind you, he was the one, the one who made it go. His act was unlike any the world had or has ever seen. What was so very special about him and his act you are wondering? Well, to begin with, this man professed to be sent by God! He willingly and openly performed unbelievable, unheard of feats of healing, compassion and love never seen before or since. And then, dear ones, for his grand finale, for the climax of his magnificent performance he did the ultimate, the unthinkable! He prostrated himself right there in that center ring and willingly offered his very life in exchange for you, for me, for the world!"

"Why would he ever do such a dramatic thing you ask? He did this that we may be free! Truly and totally free! Free of our past! Free to pursue our destiny!"

"Now, the Grand Head Ringmaster of The Greatest Show on Earth permitted this drastic finale to Jesus' act because he knew that the audience for all time, however eager and willing, was simply unable to offer suitable atonement to free them from the mire of their transgressions. They simply had not the means to do so."

Mister Goodspeak paused his lecture to allow a moment of rest. He narrowed his eyes slightly as he intently looked over the heads of the audience as if there was something there that only he could see. A precious moment, soundless but for the collective breathing of the rapt assemblage. In due time, he appropriately dropped his gaze and continued, "But my friends, this august performance didn't end there. No, no, my dears, that was truly just the very beginning. The Grand Head Ringmaster graciously restored his beloved headliner, that same Jesus, and it is His Resurrection Feast that we are so privileged to celebrate this day."

The crowd remained subdued, enraptured with Mr. Goodspeak's words. Still standing on his chair the little man carefully shuffled around as to directly face the Phikit's and their young friend. Green derby in hand he dramatically swept his arm across the throng of sideshow people as he said, "There are those among us who have much difficulty seeing the exquisite beauty and majesty of it all due to their peculiar, trying position in this present life. The infinite inclusiveness that is theirs for the offing is shrouded by one innocent walk past the house of mirrors, one chance encounter at the reflecting pool. Many seriously question, can there be any good reason for their continued existence in this hapless, hopeless struggle?"

"And then," he continued, "At the absolute perfect time, a miracle happens! The Ringmaster speaks to us! He sends his messengers into our lives, those blessed beings who show us through their many acts of kindness, that the ever present, ever abiding, miraculous love of God is not just for the bright and beautiful people of this world, but for us all!"

Mister Goodspeak concluded his message but remained standing, stone still and rock solid, head tipped back, eyes closed, smiling confidently. The little man extended his arms in front of him, palms up and murmured quietly, "Thank you."

Someone toward the back of the crowd echoed, "Thank you," then another and another followed suit. Someone laughed, several clapped and stomped, a group began to sing. And just like a distant roll of thunder on a late summer afternoon, jubilant, satisfying sounds of praise rippled through the throng. Intensifying by the very second, it became a crescendo of joy that simply could not be contained.

CONCLUSION

Some years later in another circus in a distant town, Pacha, the elephant man, had become despondent working the sideshow. He was so very tired of being gawked at and called a freak, that he had reached the absolute low point in his difficult life.

His good friend Lupus, the wolfman, told him the whole story of Phikit's Brunch. He went to unusual lengths to explain the inspiring effect it had on him and how it had saved his life and set him on his personal path to freedom.

"I love the story Lupus, but look at me, look at me!" Pacha moaned, "How or why would God even care about me?"

Lupus put his hand on Pacha's shoulder and gently squeezed. "Listen my friend," he replied, "God cares nothing about your outward appearance. Infact, He does not even see you as the world sees you. Our God searches hearts and minds to find who you truly are and if you ask He will come and make his dwelling place within you."

"Come Pacha," implored Lupus, "Heed the Ringmaster's call. Come and join The Greatest Show on Earth."

TOM'S STORY

INTRODUCTION

On a warm, late summer evening, shortly after supper, a timid tapping came at William and Minerva's farmhouse door. The ancient portal creaked in protest as an elderly, stocking footed William, coffee cup in hand, slowly pulled it open to reveal three young children standing on the stepstone. Two little boys and a girl, dressed in faded, patched clothing, old but neat and clean, just as the children.

Nobody spoke so, with an effort, William lowered his tall frame to the door sill and sat facing the three. Realizing his size and explosion of white hair and mustache could be intimidating, he half turned and called, "Minnie, come please, we have company."

In a minute Minnie appeared, aglow in the soft evening light, framed in the doorway, wiping her hands on her ever-present apron. She lightly sat down beside her husband and spoke softly to the children, "Lovely evening for a walk, isn't it?"

"We're the Drexlers!" the girl blurted out.

William and Minnie nodded and replied in unison, "Yes, yes and thank you for coming to visit."

Another long pause and the youngest, a little boy broke in, "We bin stealin!"

William leaned forward toward the trio, scowled and replied in mock seriousness, "Stealing what and from whom?"

The girl began to tear up as she spoke, "We been stealin from your gardens and momma says for us to fess up."

"But, but we only stealed, cause we was hungry," the boy pleaded.

William leaned back against the jam and turned towards Minnie saying, "Whatta think momma?"

But he was a little late as Minnie had already been to the kitchen and was on her way back. Cradled in her arm was an egg basket covered in cheese cloth and steeped in the undeniable smell of fresh baked yeast bread.

She sat on the sill, handed the basket to the girl as she gently instructed, "Tell your momma I'll be by tomorrow morning, after milking."

"Oh, and by the way," William added, holding out an empty basket retrieved from the door side, "Stop by the bean patch on your way home, these late rains have it really looking good this year."

That was William and Minnie. True people of the heart in the purest sense of the word, wanting and expecting nothing in return but goodwill and grace. They raised a half- dozen children, adopted children, grand- children and the occasional itinerant who knocked on the door to their old farmhouse set deep in the cove. They reveled in the opportunity to help, to strive for the good and perfect deed.

There are so many stories I could tell you about Will and Minnie. Let me tell you one of my favorites. Let me tell you:

TOM'S STORY.

TOM'S STORY

Part One

"Tom's got cancer," the boy's mother said it flat and matter of factly. She stood with her back to the boy, staring out the window over the sink, up to her wrists in soapy water.

"Everybody knows that," the boy thought, "Nothin new there, Tom's had the cancer for a long time now." He continued to eat his oatmeal methodically, cautiously anticipating mom's next installment, sure to come.

It was so still and quiet in the large country kitchen. The only company was the sizzle of the coal stove where the boy's mother was heating water.

After a long and motionless pause, she broke the silence again, "Heard him last night, pitiful, just pitiful. Sittin in the barnyard cryin and cryin, from the pain and all I guess."

Now, that did strike a chord with the boy and he paused, the spoon still in his mouth. One night about a week ago he had gone outback to the privy and the recollection made a lump of oatmeal stick in his throat. Hard enough to get down under the best of circumstances, it became nearly impossible when you suddenly went dry. He began to choke dangerously so he grabbed for the milk pitcher as he relived the experience.

It must have been somewhere between ten and midnight when he felt the need arise. Clad only in his customary sleeping shorts, he paused at the door and slipped his bare feet in to a pair of work shoes. Careful not to disturb his folks, he gently unlatched the screen door and stepped out onto the stoop and into the cool of the night.

It was one of those soft, summer evenings with little breeze and a brilliant harvest moon. The youngster stood very still, enjoying the night air and its refreshing feeling. He paused as he turned the corner of the house to head out back.

What in the world was that? Something very strange was in the air, strange and unnerving for sure! The boy, straining to make sense of it, finally determined odd sounds mixing with the breeze emanating from Grandpa's barn yard about a hundred paces away.

An eerie feeling set in and he resolved to ignore it all and go about his business, but the lure was strong and before he knew it, he was moving slowly and uneasily in the direction of the sound.

At the back of the barn the weird noises grew louder and louder, raising the hair on the nape of his neck. Cautiously, he slid along the side of the barn towards the front of the building.

Something in the back of the lad's brain warned him not to, but he had to know so he craned his neck and peered around the corner of the barn, empty save for the drift and sway of the shadows.

But wait, it wasn't empty! Grandma's old milking stool sat next to the barn door. There, grossly bloated and misshapen head turned sideways and tilted upward so his only eye could fix on the moon, sat Tom, moaning, moaning and moaning.

The boy had seen Tom daily for years and had sorrowfully watched as the growing cancer slowly but surely consumed him. The entire side of his head and face was now one indistinguishable cancerous growth, pulsating and frightening, for as the cancer progressed, Tom's manner and disposition regressed. It had grown to the point now that when he turned that hulking head to the side and riveted you with his one wild, wide open eye, it was enough to fill you with revulsion.

The scene that night absolutely froze the boy and he shivered in spite of the warm evening air. Bile rose in his throat as the need to escape overwhelmed him. Stepping backward, he caught his foot on a clump of sod and stumbled. He quickly regained his balance and just as quickly became aware that Tom had become silent. It was chilling and the boy didn't know what to do so, venturing a quick peek around the corner he was shocked to find Tom, still sitting on the stool, staring right back at him.

Poor old Tom was irritated and resented the intrusion on his private time, as he stared with that one unblinking eye, the boy was mesmerized. The two stood facing one another for what seemed a lifetime until the grating sound of Grandma's front door opening and closing broke the spell.

Down the path from the house to the barn came Grandma, lantern swinging rhythmically with her slow, halting steps. As she approached Tom turned and focused his eye, which had suddenly lost its glare, on grandma.

"Come Tommy," she called in her soft, whispery voice, "Let's go to the house hon."

Obediently, Tom slid from the stool and followed Grandma to the house stealing a quick backward glance every few steps.

The boy stood in the shadows around the corner of the barn for some time, glad that Grandma hadn't seen him and would never know that he had been there.

Part Two

The oatmeal, lumpy, dry and merely palatable at its very best, no longer held any appeal to the boy. He dropped his spoon and stared at his mom's back through the bottom of the jar he was using for a milk glass wondering why her dialog had taken such a tack.

"What the devil's really on her mind," he thought.

The answer wasn't long in coming and came as a complete, shocking revelation when it did!

"Son, we need to do somethin for him and for Grandma too, we need to and we must! Just can't stand to see him wastin away and going down- hill and takin Grandma with him," Mom explained.

"All well and good," the boy thought, "But what the heck can we do? Tom is what he is and Granny's never gonna turn him loose, never has, never will."

"Listen Ernie," the boy's Mom continued in earnest, "We can ease Tom's terrible sufferin and miserable existence and relieve Granny's burdened mind as well. What if, say, what if Tom was to take a walk in the wood one day and just, just never come back?"

To say that Ernie was astounded would be an understatement! He wanted to speak but couldn't, he tried to shout but no words would come!

Instead, he stood mutely as Mom outlined her plan, "I'll distract Grandma with some cookin, cannin questions or somethin like that tomorrow, while you lure Tom up the hill and into the wood. In a day Grandma will go lookin so make sure she doesn't find anything. You can do this son, I know you can. In about a week Grandma will be convinced Tom simply wandered off and ain't comin back. The poor, tortured woman will get some rest and peace of mind finally after all these years of futile carin. It will be a grand and wonderful thing to do for her and for Tom as well."

146

It was still quiet in the kitchen but the intensity was so high it was stifling as Mom continued, "Go on now, make your plan as to how you're gonna handle your end of it. I gotta get supper started."

Part Three

Now to say that Ernie was shocked to the core by the prospects of ushering Tom from this world and into eternal comfort would be an over statement. The only thing he was worried about was Grandma. How would she respond? What if she didn't go to Momma's as planned? What if she decided to go for a walk in the wood instead? What if she found out the truth? What if she found out the truth about him?

The pitiful lad was overwhelmed with what ifs as he sat, buried inside a hay stack at the edge of the hayfield. It was hot, dry and buggy and he itched, fidgeted and scratched as he mulled over his prospects.

Ernie knew full well that Tom, bold and cocksure as he was, would follow the trail of goodies he had carefully lain out for him from Grandma's, through the wood to the hay field where he lay in wait. All he had to do was bide his time and be stealthily patient.

"How in the world did we get here?" he mused, deep in reflection.

And as he waited, he wandered back, back through the years to the very beginning of it all.

Part Four

Pretty Lady had a big day that day. She proudly presented Grandma with five beautiful, healthy kittens, and Tom. Poor, poor, ugly, disfigured Tom. Pretty Lady carefully cleaned and inspected her squirming, sightless brood and began the process of nursing. All of them of course, except Tom. Her instincts told her Tom was seriously flawed and not worth the effort. She refused to touch his head with the big knot on the side or let him near the other nursing kits. With the swipe of a paw, Tom was permanently evicted and banned from nursing.

Minerva stood with her husband William and the two sorrowfully looked on.

"It's nature's way momma," William responded to Minnie's hurt and saddened look as he bent to pick up the doomed kitten.

It was only Grandma's hand on his forearm and the magic in her voice as she urged, "No William, please, no," that blessed Tom with more than the one day of life he had already painfully endured.

Minnie tried again and again to position Tom for feeding but Pretty Lady just wouldn't allow it, not even at hind tit.

The day wore on and William left to do his chores leaving Minnie to fuss alone. Poor Tom was crying in earnest now so Grandma resolved to correct things on her own, once and for all, and she headed directly for her milking station.

Minnie carefully selected a pair of old rubber gloves. Placing the open end of one to her lips, she blew into it as hard as she could, testing for leaks. Satisfied it was sound, she punched a little hole in the closed end of one of the fingers and tied off the others. Then with Bessie's help, she filled the glove with warm cow's milk. When the makeshift meal was offered to Tom the famished kitten took to it avidly.

And so, that's how it went. From that day forward Tom and Minnie became inseparable.

"Come Tommy boy," she would call when she went milking and there would be her shadow.

For his part, Tom fixed on Grandma as the only living being in his entire world who cared a whit whether he lived or didn't, and he was absolutely right! You see, as he grew and got very strong and quick, the cancer grew also and his disposition worsened. All the other barn dwellers, including Pretty Lady, grew wary of Tom and did their best to avoid him. Eventually it got to the point that when Tom's painful cancer gave him a break and he sat in the middle of the barn yard, eye partially open, quietly sunning, even the hounds would tuck tail and slink along giving him a wide berth.

At one time or another nearly every barn yard resident felt the sting of Tom's claws powered by his sheer wrath and terrible resentment. He refused to accept his lot in life graciously.

Grandma was well aware of Tom's deportment but she mercifully chalked it all up to his difficult position in life. As you would expect, she continued to shower him with affection. She bathed his ugly wound regularly and coated it with merthiolate to ward off infection. Deep down in her soul, I think she knew the battle was hopeless and most likely Tom knew it too but they did the only thing they knew to do. They carried on because, well, because for both of them it was the effort and the hope that sprang from it that made them worthy.

Part Five

Ernie and Tom enjoyed a very special relationship, they shared a bond like no other. They hated one another passionately!

It all started one day when Tom, in his peculiar state of mind, must have felt that Grandma was showing her grandson a little too much attention and affection and he didn't like it, not one bit!

"I don't think Tom likes me Grandma, look at how he glares at me," the lad complained.

"Ernie, my child, Tom's lot is difficult, we must give him some room," was Minnie's reply.

"Right, all this from a person who considers every living thing God's creation, even spiders and snakes," thought Ernie, "How she can like that mean, miserable cat I'll never Know."

In a while Tom boldened and he got to looking for opportunities to swipe at Ernie and it made the boy edgy for sure. Cleaning out the stalls in the morning, Ernie would stop for a breather and there would be Tom behind him, head cocked sideways, just giving him the bad eye, a really nasty look. Carrying milk to the spring house Ernie would close and latch the door and when he looked up, there was Tom, same ugly look on his half face.

"I'm telling you Grandma Tom hates me and I'm getting where I don't like him very much if at all," was Ernie's lament.

"Ah, Ernie, my child, try treating Tom with a little love and respect," Minnie replied, "He'll come around, you'll see."

"I'll show him love and respect, at his wake," thought the boy.

As the situation between the two foes wore on it quite naturally began to escalate. When Tom got too near, Ernie would grab a stick or a stone and toss it his way. Tom would back off just out of throwing range and give him the evil eye.

Occasionally the boy would get careless and the gap betwixt would close dangerously and, quick as lightning, the claws would flash. The poor lad's shins were taking a terrible beating.

Now it stands to reason that a fermenting situation such as this just had to have a grand finale and of course, as you have guessed, just as sure as a change in the weather, it wasn't long in coming.

Part Six

The ground level on Minnie and William's old farm house was the working area in the home. The ceiling and support stanchions were all open beam design. The lintels above the doors and windows were also open and uncovered and it was here, in these private places that Tom, when he was able, liked to take his naps. It was the perfect place for him, up and away from everything, everybody and the world.

One gloomy, rainy Saturday afternoon Tom was taking siesta on the lintel above the main door. With a swish and a bang Ernie flung the door wide calling loudly, "Hey Grandma, hey Grandpa, come on and look, the crick's floodin!"

William and Minnie called back from the canning kitchen, "Come give us a hand Ernie, we'll look in a minute!"

Ernie removed his hat and slicker and was bent over busily unbuckling his arctics. Well above him, furtively and silently, Tom cocked his massive head bringing his one eye into focus and peered down from his high perch. Low and ever more behold, there just scant feet away and directly below him was the bare, tender, unprotected neck of his hated enemy! The despoiler, the love stealer, the one being standing between his beloved Minerva and him! Old Tom came as close as he would ever come in his entire life to purring in contentment. His nemesis had been delivered into his hands or in this case and better yet, into his claws.

The pounding of the rain and the rush of the flooding crick were completely drowned out as, "AARRRROUGGGGGHHHHH," came the fierce, wild, unearthly cry as it tore from the twisted lips of Tom's grotesque half mouth! He launched himself into the air, a killing strike, a missile of doom, all four legs spread eagled, claws unsheathed, itching for action!

Ernie didn't know at first what the heck had happened but he did in a skinny minute as Tom hit his bare neck hard and dug in with a vengeance!

"AIIEEEOOWWWWEEEE," screamed the poor lad as he blindly groped and grasped Tom by the scruff of the neck. The two rolled and rolled across the floor flailing, kicking, scratching, biting, punching, cursing and screeching! Man oh man what a sight!

As the battle scene careened through the house, Ernie loosened his grip for a second to take a better swing and Tom got ready to slash again when he spied Minnie standing in the canning kitchen doorway with a stern look and a pointed index finger. The object of his adoration looked unhappy so Tom quickly broke off the engagement and fled to Minnie's feet as Ernie's best and final swing caught nothing but air!

Grandma's stern look faded as she said, "Now, now you boys cut that out, cut it out right now you hear!"

Sitting in the middle of the floor with tears in his eyes and a bleeding neck the distressed lad gasped, "See, I told ya Tom hates me Grandma, look he's laughin at me!"

By gosh if you looked closely it sure as heck seemed that Tom's half mouth was cocked in a devilish, mocking grin!

Part Seven

Ernie was having a terrible time trying to keep from sneezing as he crouched inside the bone-dry haystack waiting for Tom to show. He had a bitter taste in his mouth as he thought about how he had gotten to this point in his young life. The thing that prodded him forward however was the realization that once and forever more he was going to bury his differences with that lousy, miserable excuse for a cat.

The lad didn't know how much longer he could tolerate the conditions inside the haystack as he took the last swallow from the water jug he had brought with him. As he lowered the jug he thought he saw movement just inside the tree line. He wiped the sweat from his eyes and squinted hard and sure enough he could just barely make out a shape within the shadow of the wood. He was sure it had to be Tom, cautious as ever.

And then, there he was, following the trail of chicken parts Ernie had strategically left for him. Tom finally emerged from the dark of the wood into the bright, sunny hayfield, sniffing with his half nose, searching for one more piece of chicken.

"This is it!" hissed Ernie through clenched teeth and pursed lips as he crouched in ambush, unconsciously fingering the scars on the back of his neck, "Goodbye you lousy, miserable, no good, hateful cat!"

And with that, he pushed the rifle's safety to the off position and squeezed the trigger. But he made one very big, colossal, dumb as a rock mistake! Instead of gently easing the safety off, in his zest, he gave it a resounding click to the left!

Now, old tough as nails and wary Tom hadn't lived as long as he had by being slow and stupid. In fact, in the interval between the click of the safety and the roar of the rifle, he lived a lifetime. Truly, at the very front end of the very first click, Tom recognized the sound, knew the omen, and bolted! By the time the speeding projectile arrived in deadly earnest he had spun in his tracks and was on his way. When the blistering hot shell grazed his side from back to front he was already at top speed and as the pain added stimulation he went into hyper-drive!

KABAAAMMM! A lightning strike of orange, into the wood, down the path and gone, straight toward Grandma's!

"OH NOOOO!" bellowed Ernie as he burst from the haystack in frantic pursuit. In a minute he was flying, elbows and knees pumping high, feet barely touching ground, with a trail of hay, grass and dust streaming behind, but the unfortunate lad wasn't even in the same league as Tom. Where speed was concerned the two shouldn't be mentioned in the same breath.

By the time the boy shot from the wood at the top of the orchard, gasping, panting, spitting and coughing, Tom was already at the foot of the hill groveling at Grandma's feet.

Minnie had thoroughly enjoyed coffee with her daughter and was in a pleased mood as she walked home taking a shortcut through the barnyard. When Tom spotted her he immediately fled straight to his protector screeching, wailing and crying pitifully! At first Grandma thought it was the cancer acting up again until Tom showed her his side and the stinging, ugly, red streak running back to front, the poor woman was aghast!

From his vantage point at the very top of the orchard Ernie was bent double, elbows on knees and mouth wide open sucking wind when he saw Minnie reach down, cradle Tom in her arms and, with her head on a swivel, make for the house as fast as she was able.

"Oh no," the distraught lad moaned, "What's going to happen now?"

Part Eight

"Maybe South Carolina or even California or Tennessee," Ernie thought, "No, no Alaska, that's it! I'll pike out for Alaska right now, nobody will ever find me there, not even Grandma! Now, which way is Alaska? Oh man, I don't even know which way to go, what's going to happen now," wailed poor, poor Ernie as he cried from his pit of despair.

The sorrowful lad flopped down in the grass and cradled his head in his hands. As he sat glumly staring down the hill toward William and Minnie's place he suddenly jerked and gave a start.

"What was that?" he whispered, "Did someone peek around the corner of the house?" "Yeah, oh yeah, someone is there for sure. They're sneaking a look around the corner. They're looking for something. No, they're looking for someone. Man oh man, they're looking for the shooter, yeah, they're looking for me!"

"It's Grandma, I know it is and she sees me, look, she's staring at me, she's glaring at me! But wait, she can't see this far she has katarack eyes, she can't see way up here! But what does she see? What's she gaping at? Yeah, oh yeah she sees me, for sure, oh no!"

And just that quickly, the mysterious head disappeared. Was it really Minnie? Did she somehow manage to eye Ernie way up there at the top of the orchard? The poor lad thought so. In fact, he was sure of it and the very notion dragged his spirits ever lower.

"Well, that's it," the boy mumbled as he shook his head slowly from side to side in distress. "That's it, I've crossed that line, the Grandma line. That's it, I'm done, done for sure, no help for me. There's no turning back, not for me, I'm finished, it's over."

As the pitiful lad sat, arms clenched around and head resting upon drawn up knees, it didn't look as if it could get any worse for him. When a shadow ominously loomed over him, he knew that it had just gotten worse, very much worse. William was a tall man with a mass of bristling white hair and a flowing mustache. As he stood in front of Ernie, blocking out the sun, from ground level he looked absolutely monumental.

"Hi Grandpa, what cha doin?" murmured Ernie, trying to sound off handed.

"Ah Ernie, Grandma says someone took a crack at poor old Tom, not that I blame them you know. His disposition and manners have gone to seed of late. Asked me to scout up this way and take a good look, see if the shooter might a left any sign, you know how she is about Tom," William replied.

She's down home patchin him up, why don't you go give her a hand, I'll be along shortly," William called over his shoulder as he walked into the wood.

Ernie winced visibly as he thought, "Go give her a hand! Ohh nooo! I'm a gonner, a gonner for sure!"

Part Nine

Grandma was sitting on the large stepstone at the ground floor entrance, fussing over Tom when Ernie came round the corner of the house. Deep down Tom began a low rumbling growl that quickly accelerated into a vicious snarl as the boy approached. Minnie tightened her grip on the tough, rangy feline and he settled some but not very much.

"Hi Grandma, what's goin on?" Ernie asked in his most nonchalant voice.

You see, as the desperate boy had scuffed on down the hill through the orchard, hands thrust deep in his pockets, head down, he made a dramatic decision on how he would handle this direst of situations. He knew he had but one strand of hope upon which to cling. He was about to attempt the bluff, the big bluff, in fact, the biggest most perfect bluff of the century! To pull it off would require a certain flair, a debonair attitude that he was desperately working to acquire.

"Good gosh amighty Grandma, what happened to Tom? He queried in his most considerate and apprehensive voice.

Minnie sat motionless staring at the nervous lad, one arm around Tom's neck, her rheumy eyes flooded with tears. A curious look clouded her face as she sniffed the air, turning her head slightly.

"Oh no," Ernie thought, "She smells gun smoke, she smells it on me! Oh no, I'm a gonner now, a gonner for sure!"

Minnie cut the boy's line of thought and broke the silence as well as she responded to everyone and no one in particular in a soft, musical voice set on sad,

"If I live to be a hundred, I will never understand the utter meanness in the world. I don't think it was ever meant to be this way. Just when you think all is well the enemy strikes at you viciously, with all he has. What did we do to deserve this? What did poor Tom do? Rejected by his own from birth, all he wants is to struggle through his difficult life with someone to care for him, with someone to care about him, perhaps even to love him a little, that's all. Is that too much to ask? Is that too much for him? Is he not worthy of even that much compassion?"

There was nothing more to say. Ernie had no intelligent response. He just stood there, open mouthed, a confused look on his face, the wind of debonair gone completely. Tears formed at the corners of his eyes and glistened on his cheeks. At the sight, true to her given nature, Minnie's demeanor softened and she gently urged her grandson down on the stone beside her. He was devastated by Minnie's soliloquy and began to blubber in earnest.

Minnie wrapped a slender, delicate arm around Ernie's neck, just as she had Tom and with surprising strength pulled his head down to her lap, just as she had Tom. She turned her head to the side and gently placed it atop the two and there they were, the three seemingly at perfect peace.

Underneath it all Ernie squirmed and squirmed until he was directly facing Tom who scrooched and scrooched till he was facing Ernie with his one bulging eye. The old foes bore in on one another with a passion. Ernie frowned and produced his ugliest grimace, his eyes narrowed to slits and he stuck out his tongue. Tom growled, snarled and whined, he bared his fangs and spit at Ernie who quickly spat back. And so, face to half face, eyeball to eyeball they fought a silent battle of glares, contortions and spittle as Minnie began to hum and then to quietly, gently sing in her peculiar, heartfelt, melodic way.

"Hmm hmmm, hmm hmmm, how sweeeeet the sound, that saved a wretch like meeee. I once was lost but now I'm found, was blind but now I seeeeee."

Part Ten

The sun had slowly waned and the shadows grown long by the time William emerged from the wood behind his daughter's house. Together they sat on the stoop and talked awhile about the day and the effect it would have on all.

In a little while William took his daughter's hand and they walked together to the home stead in search of the three. That's when they found them, Minnie, Ernie and Tom, still huddled together on the stepstone, the picture of tranquility, all fast asleep.

The sun was brilliantly setting in a last show of glory as William and Dorothy pulled the sawhorse close up to the house and sat on it. Neither was anxious to alter the serenity of the scene after the day's hectic events.

"After all," they thought, "When all the peace and forgiveness has grown thin and fallen away, who knows what tomorrow will bring?"

Conclusion

The battle was over but the war certainly was not. Tom and Ernie did their best to avoid heavy, open conflict. Not because they wanted mind you, they did it for the sake of Minnie whom they both dearly loved in their own special way.

However, out of sight and sound, the war of sticks and stones and fang and claw wore on.

About two years after Tom's near encounter with eternity, he sat in the center of the barnyard one day, sunning, as life revolved about him. Turning his massive head side to side he worked to source an uncommon sound that wafted about.

The wood line at the top of the orchard stretched away into the distance and it was here that Tom eventually fixed his one bulging eye. Then, without a single backward glance, he rose and with head drooping, slowly plodded up the hill toward the dark, cool forest atop.

It seemed that after living near the edge all those years old Tom just naturally knew when to go. Minnie knew it too. She knew it in the way Tom curled himself around her ankle that morning at milking, something he never did. She knew and she accepted it as one of the myriad, mystical events that occur in the natural order of things.

For her part though, Minerva never forgot her precious Tom and his valiant struggle for life. She talked long and often of his strength, courage and perseverance.

You can bet that Tom, wherever he is, talks often of Grandma. I'm certain the saints and angels do.

www.ingramcontent.com/pod-product-compliance
Lightning Source LLC
Chambersburg PA
CBHW020620250626
47154CB00004B/1602